Stand Out in a Crowd

Cupar Old Parish Church

Presented to

Lorna Kirkhope

June 1988

[signature]

Minister

". . . we have peace with God
through our Lord Jesus Christ."
Romans 5:1

Christian Literature Press – Cwmbran   (Teal Press Ltd)

Stand Out in a Crowd

Gail Vinall

Scripture Union
130 City Road, London EC1V 2NJ

© Gail Vinall 1987
First published 1987

ISBN 0 86201 455 7

Phototypeset by Input Typesetting Ltd., London
Printed and bound in Great Britain by Cox and Wyman
Ltd., Reading

1

Rachel watched the string of lights curling up and over the next hill as the car sped down the motorway. It was still raining. The windscreen wipers flicked to and fro almost in time with the beat of the record on the radio. Every fourth beat they edged ahead and then, a few seconds later, the music somehow caught up and both were beating in harmony again. A towering motorway sign flashed by, bearing familiar place names.

The week had gone so quickly. Her father would soon be turning off the motorway and then Rachel would be back home with her mum. Would her father come in for a while? Probably not. He had to drive back up the motorway tonight to his new home in the Midlands . . . and Ann. What a strange week it had been. It hadn't turned out at all as Rachel had anticipated.

She remembered all the hassle of just persuading her mum to let her spend this week away in the first place; then meeting Ann, the woman her father was now living with. The three of them had done so much together. There had been crazy picnics in the rain, the trip on the canal boat, the shopping spree, and her dad getting cross about the parking ticket. Checking for the third time since the beginning of the journey, Rachel slid her hand into her pocket to feel the tiny box containing the pink earrings which her dad had bought her. It was still safely there.

'OK?' her dad asked.

'Yes, thanks. How much longer will we be?'

'Only about twenty minutes.'

'Are you coming in?'

'No love, not tonight. Your mum and I sorted everything out when I picked you up. It's best if I just drop you off and get on back.'

It's a long way, Rachel thought. Still, Ann would be waiting up for him. Rachel had been determined to hate her but that had been impossible. Ann had been kind, and a lot of fun. A whole week, and there hadn't been a single row or even a nasty word between them. For years Rachel had assumed that having parents who constantly argued was a normal state of events.

This time last week Rachel had felt really nervous about going to her dad's new home and now she felt equally anxious about coming back.

When they pulled up in the drive Rachel saw the net curtains twitch upstairs and guessed that her mum was watching, maybe expecting to see Ann.

'I've had a lovely time, Dad,' Rachel said.

'It's been great, darling. I'll see you after term ends and then you'll come up for a fortnight. We'll go on that camping trip.'

'Lovely,' Rachel said, trying to sound bright.

She leaned across to kiss her dad. He held her tightly and then reached across to open the door. Rachel put her anorak hood up and clambered out. Her father carried her bags to the front door.

'Got your key?' he asked.

'Yes it's here,' Rachel said, fumbling in her shoulder bag. It seemed strange that her dad should be standing in front of what had been his home for years and yet not have the key to open the front door. There was an awkward pause and then he squeezed her arm briefly.

'Right then, I'll be in touch soon. Be good, darling,' her father said, and then he was gone. The car drove away, leaving Rachel shivering in the cold, damp air.

As she struggled into the hall, her mum appeared from the kitchen. She kissed Rachel and then hovered uncertainly.

'Has your dad gone?' she asked anxiously.

'Yes, he couldn't stay.'

'Did he say anything?'

'Only about the rates.'

'Oh yes – good. Well, have you had a nice time?' her mother dutifully enquired.

'Fantastic, Mum – we've been all over the place and . . .' Rachel hesitated, suddenly afraid of seeming to have enjoyed being away. 'It was good,' she ended quietly.

'What is your dad's house like?'

'Oh it's sweet – really cosy. The bedroom he decorated for me is ever so pretty . . .'

'Hm, he never liked decorating when he was here. Still, I expect there's an incentive now.'

Rachel sighed. It was useless trying to have a normal conversation with her mum if it involved her dad. She wandered through to the kitchen and poured herself some milk. Mrs Vaughan followed her.

'Well, did you meet Ann?'

'Yes, I met her,' Rachel replied offhandedly.

'And?'

'And what?' Rachel cried, exasperated.

'What is she like?'

'Well – nice, Mum, to be honest.'

'Oh.' The disappointment was impossible to miss.

'No doubt you've been spoilt to death. Well, I hope you haven't come home expecting the same treatment here. Goodness knows I can't afford treats and presents.'

'Mum! Nobody bought me presents,' Rachel cried, and then guiltily remembered the earrings. Oh well, she wouldn't mention them just yet. 'I've had a lovely time and now I'm glad to be back with you.'

'Some glamorous little madam I expect,' her mum continued, almost to herself. 'What she sees in your father I'll never know but it won't last. He'll be back, and then we'll see who's gloating . . .'

'Nobody's gloating, Mum,' Rachel interrupted. 'She's not glamorous and Dad's not living the high life or anything. He likes his new home and I'm glad.'

'Oh, that's right – you take his side now. My own daughter turning against me!'

Rachel said softly, 'I'm tired, Mum, I think I'll get up to bed.'

Rachel brooded moodily as she unpacked and rearranged her room that evening. It was impossible to please adults. They were always telling you not to be childish and then, when it came down to it, they behaved worse than most kids. If it was going to cause all these problems she'd almost prefer not to see her dad. Well, no – she wanted desperately to see him. Life was difficult sometimes!

The next morning was Sunday and Rachel woke to hear her mum bustling around downstairs. Rachel rolled over in bed and lay thinking for a few minutes.

Church. The idea wasn't depressing but there again it wasn't that exciting either. At least Vanessa, her best friend, would be there so she could catch up on the week's news. Paul would be taking the Bible class this week, which was good because he was usually interesting. Andy would be there too – which reminded her, she must return the book he'd lent her. Where had she put it?

Andy was always lending her Christian books or tapes. Rachel usually accepted them politely but she didn't always read or listen to them. Andy was quite sweet really. He liked her, and made the fact quite obvious. Rachel smiled to herself. He wasn't her idea of a boyfriend but still, it was quite flattering to be paid so much attention. Then there were the others.

Carole would be there in a new top or skirt, saying, 'Oh, I just picked it up down the market.' Rachel wished she had a Saturday job and was able to buy pretty clothes. Carole's brother, Mike, would be talking about his new rock group, and Mandy would be egging him on because she was hoping he'd ask her to join as vocals.

Rachel sighed. It would have been nice, just once, to have missed church and spent the day doing something totally different. When her father had been at home they had gone to the Baptist church in town fairly regularly but just recently Mrs Vaughan had been almost ferocious in her attendance. Rachel had no idea why her mum was so keen nowadays but there was no arguing with her.

Rachel frowned as she started to dress, choosing her scruffiest jeans and a T-shirt. There was a slight pleasure in this small act of rebellion.

Sometimes at school people asked her and Vanessa why they went to church. Vanessa always replied, 'To worship and to learn more about God,' but Rachel felt uncomfortable if she had to give a reason because, to be perfectly honest, she hadn't really worked out why she did go.

It was partly because they'd always gone, as a family. You sort of got into the habit. There were many people there who had known her since she was a baby and they meant a lot to her. She liked Paul Gould, their teacher, because he was fun, and his wife was nice too. God was obviously important to these people and the way they lived.

Rachel felt rather vague about her own idea of God. She loved the stories Jesus had told in the Bible and the things he had said to people. Jesus was a special character and Rachel experienced a mixture of feelings as she read about him. There were times when he was heroic and powerful, and then at other times he seemed so sad and lonely.

But the thing Rachel couldn't work out was what difference it made to her everyday life. She understood in theory why Jesus had died and she appreciated that many of his rules made a lot of sense, but plenty of people who weren't Christians thought so too. It was the notion of having some sort of relationship with God that baffled her.

Then there was the whole business of prayer. Of course, you didn't just ask for things like a shopping list. It had to be what God would want – but surely God would have wanted her mum and dad to stay together, and she'd prayed really hard that they would. Then she'd prayed that Ann wouldn't make her dad happy so he'd come back, but Ann *had* made him happy and now Rachel had started to like her as well! What a joke. Where did that leave God and prayer? It was a mystery. So why was she going to church that morning? Rachel couldn't have answered.

2

The morning service began at eleven o'clock but a last-minute panic over the automatic switch on the cooker meant that Rachel and her mum arrived breathlessly as the choir were finishing their anthem. They filed in just before the prayers and had to sit in the front row. Rachel never could understand why people always sat at the back in churches.

While their minister led the prayers, Rachel gazed around the building, only half-listening. The front wall was painted blue, and dominated by the gaunt black cross hanging mysteriously in the dusky gloom. Above it was a circular stained-glass window. The sun was shining through it, and the eyes in the face of Jesus were piercingly bright. They seemed to be looking straight at Rachel. It gave her a strange feeling. Rachel caught a phrase of the prayer suddenly, 'God has the power to make a man whole' – God has the power to make a manhole. She felt her shoulders shake and suddenly emitted a snort of laughter as the phrase repeated itself in her mind. Mrs Vaughan shot her a look so Rachel coughed and dived into her shoulder bag for a mint.

Rachel glanced down at her mum's bowed head. There were more grey hairs now than she remembered. Mrs

Vaughan didn't use her rinse so frequently these days. She looked tired and her lips were mouthing words silently.

Suddenly, Rachel felt a rush of tenderness for her, and moved closer so that she could lean against her arm.

After the weekly notices the organist started up the hymn and it was time for the young people to file away into the hall for their classes. Rachel liked sitting in the church but she was pleased to leave now for the more informal atmosphere of her own class.

They waited outside one of the church offices chatting noisily, until Paul Gould arrived, pulling a bunch of keys from his pocket.

'Hi all!' he beamed.

They jostled into the room which was the minister's office for the rest of the week. It was very untidy, littered with books and papers, but cheerful and pleasant. Out of the windows you could look over the rooftops of the neighbouring shops and houses right out to the estuary.

Paul pulled a packet of biscuits out of one pocket to pass round, and pens and paper from another. Eventually everyone had sorted out a pen which contained ink and found something to rest on. Rachel was babbling away to Vanessa so eagerly that she missed the first biscuit round completely.

'Right! Are we all set?' Paul asked at last. 'Good, now we're picking up the theme of forgiveness again this week and looking at the story of the woman caught in adultery. So could you all turn up that page . . .'

There was a general flipping of pages. Andy immediately noticed that Rachel had forgotten her Bible and offered her his but she smiled and said she would share with Vanessa.

Paul started to read the passage. In fact, Rachel knew the story well; it was one of her favourites. She loved the picture of the poor defenceless woman and the crowd of bitter men all shouting and longing to throw their stones at her, while Jesus sat there so calmly, drawing in the sand. Rachel always wondered just what he had been drawing. He had known, so cleverly, how to save the woman and at the same time show the crowd how hypocritical they were being.

'Well, now,' Paul began, 'what really strikes you about this story?'

After a moment's reflection Rachel volunteered, 'It really put those rotten men in their places! Good for Jesus.'

Paul smiled, impressed as usual by her spontaneous response.

'She learnt her lesson without having to pay for it,' Vanessa added seriously.

'Yes, that's a good point,' Paul agreed.

'Well, Jesus knew she wouldn't sin again in that way,' Andy put in.

'I don't think he *knew* at all,' Rachel returned. 'He trusted her not to sin again, that's all. He wouldn't have let her be stoned even if he'd known she *was* going to commit adultery again.'

'I don't see how you can say that. After all, the sin *does* matter, even if Jesus lets her off,' Andy argued.

'It probably doesn't matter half as much as all the anger the crowd felt towards her,' Carole said.

'Exactly!' Rachel pronounced.

'What I think we're saying,' Paul said, 'is that this passage is much more to do with forgiveness and tolerance than about judging any particular sin.'

'But that's like saying that it doesn't matter who does what so long as we all forgive each other!' Andy interrupted.

Rachel opened her mouth but shut it again quickly.

Come to think of it, there was a way in which that statement seemed true to her. Andy, however, might not have been impressed if she'd said so.

'Well, all right Andy, tell us a little more,' Paul encouraged.

Andy was warming to his argument. 'The Bible lays down definite rules about things like stealing, slander and . . . adultery. You can't just brush them aside.'

'Are you saying they can't be forgiven?' Rachel asked sharply.

'No, of course not,' Andy replied, 'but, well, they have to be put right, and then you forgive.'

'Oh, that's daft, Andy! If you go and kill someone you can't put that right,' Rachel scoffed. She knew she was being rather mean and tripping him up just for the sake of it, but his attitude was beginning to irritate her. Perhaps it was partly the subject, which was threatening to her. Rachel couldn't really accept that adultery was such a sin now. That would have had too many unhappy implications for her mum and dad.

'Well, anyway, I think the point of the story is the importance of not sinning again,' Andy declared stubbornly.

'Oh, what's so awful about what she did?' Rachel was almost surprised at herself, but she'd said it now.

'You can't mean that, Rachel,' Andy said. 'You're just saying it because . . .'

'Because my dad has done the same! Is that what you were going to say?'

There was a horrified pause.

'I'm sorry,' Andy said, immediately contrite.

Rachel couldn't be angry with him. 'It's all right Andy. I'm not mad about that but honestly, your ideas are – well – so black or white. You never see any grey areas, do you?'

'There shouldn't be any,' Andy said.

Rachel was silent. A voice deep inside was saying that Andy was right but how could she admit it? As Paul continued, Rachel heard Andy's words repeating themselves in her mind.

After the class had formally ended and people were just chatting she couldn't help but continue the discussion with Andy, despite his reluctance.

'No, go on, Andy, just be honest,' she said.

'Well, if people make a promise to God to stay married, then they've got to.'

'But people change!' Rachel insisted.

'The promises don't.'

'So what should people do?'

'Stay together.'

'No matter what?'

'Yes.'

'Oh, Andy, you just don't see, do you?'

'No, I don't see! I don't see why rules can't be kept when it's all plain and clear.'

'Don't you ever break rules?'

'It's a bit different from chewing gum in class!'

'But my dad's much happier than he was when he and mum were together. What's so Christian about being miserable, just for the sake of abiding by the rules?'

'The alternative is chucking all the rules!'

'Hey, you two,' Paul interrupted, 'I'm passing a list round for anyone who wants to sign up for baptism classes. We talked about it last week when you were away, Rachel. Think about it. There's no rush and no commitment at this stage. I'm just trying to find out who might be interested.'

Andy took the list and printed his name clearly, then hesitated with pen poised. 'Shall I put your name down?' he asked.

'Um, no, I'll do it later,' Rachel said.

The list passed on and Rachel saw Carole and then Vanessa sign it. If only she could be sure about things, as everyone else seemed to be. The morning's discussion had been interesting but it only helped her to feel what a gulf there was between the way she saw Christianity and how others, like Andy, saw it. Could she honestly think about taking such a step as baptism with some of the doubts in her mind? If only she could have Andy's faith.

'Sketching this afternoon?' Vanessa asked as they drifted downstairs.

'What? Oh yes, all right. Are you up at the stables first?'

'Yes, you can have a ride if you get there early.'

'No, thanks, I'll cycle up to meet you at three o'clock and we can go on down to the quay.'

'Fine – bring some food and then we needn't rush home. Must dash, dad's dying to get home for the snooker on television! See you.'

'Yeah. Bye Nessa,' Rachel said absently.

Downstairs in the main hall people were clustered in small groups drinking coffee and chatting. Mrs Vaughan was busy talking, so Rachel decided to wait outside. She smiled and waved to various people as she edged her way to the side door.

Outside the church, Rachel perched on the wall and blinked in the bright sunlight. Her mother could be another half hour but it was nice just sitting in the warmth. Rachel was day-dreaming when the sound of motorbikes revving suddenly shook her back to reality. As her eyes focussed on the group of kids surrounding the two motorbikes she recognised a girl from her class at school, called Sue, whom she knew vaguely.

Surprised, Rachel saw Sue glance in her direction and

then begin to wave. As Rachel shouted back 'Hi,' the rest of the group turned to look at her. With a jolt, Rachel recognised Steve, the owner of one of the bikes and a prefect at school in the sixth form. She hardly knew him really, but she had liked him for nearly six months. In all that time they'd only spoken a few times but just recently Rachel had had the impression that he'd shown rather more interest. It was a bit hard to tell but, if it wasn't her imagination or wishful thinking, there had been one or two occasions when he had paid her more attention than necessary. She remembered one incident in particular when the prefects had been selling tickets for the end of term disco. She and Vanessa had been queuing for ages but, what with some fourth-year boys barging in, they were still nowhere near the front when the bell for the end of lunch had rung. Disappointed, they had turned away when Steve, who was one of the ticket prefects, had called her back.

'Let Rachel have her tickets, she's been waiting long enough,' he had said to the girl collecting the money. The girl had raised an eyebrow expressively but handed Rachel the tickets as directed. Rachel had been quite taken aback at the time. She still recalled with shame how Vanessa had giggled beside her. Still, it all seemed to suggest that Steve was at least slightly interested in her. This was very flattering because he was nearly two years older than her and easily one of the best-looking boys in the sixth form.

Rachel had been out with one or two boys, in a very casual way, but mostly the boys in her year irritated her with their stupid sense of humour and awkward conversation. Steve was something else – way out of her league in fact, she told herself. It was ridiculous to think he'd even noticed her. Yet it wasn't entirely her imagination because right now he was smiling at her.

Sue called her over and Rachel slid down from the wall as gracefully as possible. She felt a little ashamed of being seen outside the church. She sauntered over to the group and said hello. There were a few titters from a couple of the girls and then Jeff, Steve's mate, called out, 'Been saying your prayers, then?'

Rachel flushed but composedly replied, 'Sort of. I'm just waiting for Mum, actually.'

'Oh, sorry for the mistake, actually!' he mimicked.

Rachel felt herself curling up inside but Steve said, 'Knock it off, Jeff,' and that was sufficient to revive her.

'We're going down the beach,' Sue volunteered. 'Steve's going to give me a ride on his bike when we get there.'

'How are you getting down?'

'Steve and Jeff are on their bikes, the rest of us are going by train.'

'That sounds fun,' Rachel commented a little wistfully.

'Yeah, well, you've got to do something on a Sunday or you end up knocking round town getting bored stiff,' Sue chatted on.

It was unusual for her to be quite this friendly but Rachel guessed that it had something to do with the fact that Sue was with Steve. It was a coveted position and she'd want to make sure as many people as possible knew, even if it was only Rachel. As she gabbled on, she sidled up to Steve and laid a hand possessively on the sleek silver side of the bike.

Rachel looked across to the church from where she expected her mum would soon be appearing. She wasn't there yet, thank goodness. As Rachel glanced back towards Sue she caught Steve's eye for a second and something jumped in her stomach. She looked away deliberately but she could feel the fierce heat in her cheeks rising.

'Hey, what're you doing this afternoon?' Steve enquired casually.

'Oh, nothing much,' Rachel replied, guiltily remembering that she was supposed to be meeting Vanessa.

'Why don't you come along, then?' he said.

Rachel was confused by the directness of the question, especially considering Sue was there, but she knew too that it was impossible to accept.

'I think Mum wants some help to mow the lawns this afternoon,' she lied glibly. It would sound creepy to say she was doing homework.

'That's that then. Come on, Steve,' Jeff said impatiently.

'Hold on,' Steve said quietly. 'Listen Rachel, we'll be back around six so if you fancy coming round to my house later, drop in and have a coffee. We'll all be there.'

'Thanks,' Rachel said, struggling to contain her excitement and appear nonchalant about the whole thing. After all, she reprimanded herself, it probably means nothing – he's just being friendly, or he wants another admirer, which was more than likely.

Abruptly, he kick-started the bike; Jeff did the same. Steve swung the silver-black machine in a curve across the road and then was gone in a cloud of noise and dust. Rachel watched as the bike growled down the road and then stood tasting the raw fumes in her mouth.

As she wandered back to the church wall, Rachel could almost have shouted out loud with excitement. She relived the brief meeting, with every word and look gaining extra significance in her imagination. Perhaps he really did like her!

Mrs Vaughan appeared and Rachel scrambled her bag and coat together, trying to appear normal. On the way home, Rachel mentioned her plans to meet Vanessa and then fell silent, her mind racing around dreams and doubts all connected with Steve.

3

As soon as lunch was cleared away Rachel slipped up to her room to sort out her pencils and sketch board. She didn't need to change but she sat in front of her dressing table mirror eyeing her reflection critically. Was she pretty or not, she tried to decide? If at all, it was probably in the fresh-faced milk advert style rather than a sultry, sophisticated way. Still, her hair was quite nice; light brown and shiny. Rachel picked up her hairbrush and began brushing her hair this way and that, adding slides and then discarding them. It looked best just loose.

Rachel then tipped out the contents of her make-up bag, and picked over the eye colours. What could she get away with tomorrow at school? Make-up was supposed to be 'discreet' but it tended to be all or nothing among the girls in her form. Suddenly remembering, Rachel scrabbled in the back of the drawer to pull out the box containing the new earrings, and put them on. They looked very pretty. Perhaps her mum wouldn't notice them.

A glance at her watch sent Rachel dashing into the wardrobe for her anorak. She'd have to cycle like fury to be at the stables on time. Rachel hammered down the stairs. Her mum was on the phone, laughing at something whoever she was speaking to had said. Rachel mouthed a silent goodbye as she passed, received a brief glance and wave, and then her mother emitted another shrill of delight and turned back to the phone.

As Rachel opened the front door she overheard her mother saying, 'Well, I'm not sure – maybe later,' in a very guarded tone and this was followed by a soft murmur which was lost. Momentarily, she wondered who her mum was speaking to but she quickly dismissed the thought. It was probably no one in particular. Rachel breathed in the clean air of a bright afternoon with rising exhilaration. She manoeuvered her bike out of the garage, dragging garden tools and a pile of flower pots out with it. Rachel toed them roughly back into position and then set off up the road.

It was good to feel the wind smacking against her coat and dragging back her hair. Rachel pumped away at the pedals and gradually picked up speed. The road up to the stables, where Vanessa's cousin kept a pony, skirted the back of the estate and climbed steadily away from the centre of the town. Houses and neat gardens rapidly gave way to fields.

Rachel persevered until the backs of her legs were aching, and then she dismounted to walk the final quarter of a mile. The stables were really two or three glorified sheds set in a small, rather dusty paddock. In winter it was a quagmire but just now it consisted of areas of tired grass and hard-baked ruts. One or two horses were standing sleepily in an adjoining field but Vanessa was nowhere in sight.

Rachel abandoned her bike and approached the stalls where she could hear noises of someone mucking out. Peering through the gloom, Rachel saw Vanessa shovelling straw and manure into a wheelbarrow. She was raising clouds of dust and the peculiar acid-sweet smell of horses hung in the air. At one end of the stall a little grey pony was tethered. It gave Rachel an evil leer as she entered.

'What an awful smell!' Rachel grimaced.

'Oh, it's you!' Vanessa returned, not looking up. 'It's not so bad when you get used to it.'

'Are you nearly finished?'

'Yes, almost. Hand me that broom.'

Rachel picked up the broom and stepped gingerly towards Vanessa, trying to avoid getting her trainers dirty.

'I'll wait outside,' she said. 'Hurry up.'

It was pleasant just sitting in the sun and Rachel was beginning to feel too lazy to move again when Vanessa finally joined her and began peeling off her overalls.

'You should have come up earlier – you could have had a canter round the field.'

'You'd have to pay me good money to get up on that little beast!' Rachel retorted.

'Oliver's sweet!' Vanessa defended him stoutly.

'He's got it in for me. I haven't forgotten last time. I don't know why your cousin doesn't sell him – preferably to a canning factory.'

'You know you don't mean that.'

'You'd be surprised. Anyway, let's get a move on or we'll never get anything done.'

'Why are people always rushing me!' Vanessa grumbled as she stuffed her things into a saddle bag and climbed onto her bicycle. Rachel grinned unsympathetically and shouted, 'Race you!'

They were soon free-wheeling back down the road into town. There was a bit of an incline near the railway station and over the bridge but then it was all downhill to the quay.

Here they dismounted and laid their bikes against the

wall before setting off, sketchboards under their arms, to find a decent vantage point.

Vanessa wanted the view south, down river to the mouth of the estuary. That way, the sky was a deep blue and the hills curled back and down out of sight. There were plenty of boats sailing up and down the river. Some of them were humble affairs; rowing boats or brightly coloured, squat little motor boats looking top heavy. There were one or two aged fishing boats chugging laboriously along with creaking timbers.

Suddenly, in the distance, heralded by a dozen or so screaming gulls, a beautiful yacht appeared with lemon-coloured sails.

'Look at that!' Rachel breathed. 'Isn't she beautiful!'

Vanessa squinted into the sun. 'Oh, fantastic. I wonder how much that's worth.'

'Thousands,' Rachel returned, not taking her eyes off the lovely craft. 'I'm going to sketch her.'

'You'll have to hurry – she's coming in at a fair old rate – the perspective will keep changing.'

Rachel ripped off the sheet she'd been doodling on and started marking lines furiously on the clean page. The boat dipped and rose with the waves, cutting a fine wake through the water. The sails rippled from the towering masts.

Minutes passed as the two girls worked in silence. Finally, Rachel stopped drawing and simply stared at the yacht dreamily. Vanessa noticed, and put down her pencil.

'Did you have a good week?' she asked.

'Yes, it was great. Why?'

'You seemed a bit off this morning. You really let rip at Andy. He was only being – well, Andy.'

'Andy's sweet really but he can be a pain.'

'Maybe, but there was no need to go for him.'

'I know – I was sorry afterwards but I wish he wouldn't carry on like that, as if he's got all the answers.'

Vanessa paused and then asked, 'Did you sign up for baptism classes?'

'No.'

'Oh, why not?'

'I don't know exactly. You did.'

'Of course.'

'You're so sure, aren't you?'

'Well, aren't you?' Vanessa replied, surprised.

'Oh yes, in a way, but other times I have so many questions and doubts that I wonder if I'm a Christian at all. Sometimes I don't even care. All I want is to have fun.'

'But we do have fun. You enjoy the youth club, don't you?'

'Oh yes. We have some laughs but . . .'

'I still don't know what you want.'

'Fun, excitement, danger!'

'Why danger for goodness' sake?'

'Just for the hell of it!'

It was an odd phrase to use but Vanessa let it pass.

'I don't know, Nessa,' Rachel continued, 'but this week really made me stop and think. There's my dad, sticking with Mum all those years because it was their duty or something and now he's with Ann, which everyone thinks is so awful, and he's happy!'

'So?'

'Well, don't you wonder sometimes whether you might be missing out on life?'

'How?'

'Well, going to church on a Sunday morning for example when you could be having a ride on a motorbike!' Rachel suggested.

'I don't like motorbikes,' Vanessa returned obtusely.

'Well, anything you *do* like then!' Rachel insisted, racking her brains for another example.

'Don't you like going to church then?'

'Oh, I don't mind it, I'm just saying there could be other things to do.'

'There are other times to do them.'

'But not with those sorts of people.'

'What people?'

'Exciting people!'

'There are some fantastic people at church.'

'But they aren't the sort of people who go out and do daring things.'

'That depends on what you call daring.'

'Maybe.'

'I don't know what you want,' Vanessa said, a little bewildered by the conversation.

'Just to have some fun, and forget about the consequences for a change.'

'I don't think you can. I reckon you'll always pay for whatever you do sooner or later. Anyway, I'm happy as I am.'

'I wish I was. Nothing exciting ever happens to me,' Rachel sighed. She opened a packet of mints and tossed one into Vanessa's lap.

'Hey, have you finished that drawing?'

'Not really, but it'll do. I can fill in the gaps at home. What about you?'

Rachel gazed at her sketch ruefully. It didn't give any of the impression of grandeur or grace that she'd been hoping to catch. Why was it that she could never put down on paper what she saw?

'I don't think I'll make an artist.'

'Let's see. Well, you could turn it upside down and say it was an abstract inspiration!'

'Very funny! And you'll back me up when I present

it to Mrs Pope of course.'

Rachel snapped the rubber bands around her folder and stood up.

'Let's have something to eat.'

'OK.'

They shared their packed teas and then wandered further along the quay to take in another view. Time slipped away and they made their way back into town until their paths diverged.

'See you tomorrow,' Rachel said.

'Yeah. Bye.'

When Vanessa was out of sight Rachel turned off from her usual route and headed in the direction of Steve's house. Once she was in sight of his house, she stopped uncertainly, remembering his invitation to coffee. Had he really meant it, she wondered? If only she could be like other people – just bang on the front door and attack the situation! But no, she couldn't do that. Anyway, she'd be late home and her mum would start to worry. She stopped, hidden behind some bushes, and glanced up at Steve's house. There was a hum of pop music from an upstairs window and some voices, which meant the others would still be there. She could go in, just say she'd been passing and heard them. But that would be horribly pushy. No, she couldn't possibly knock on the door. She walked on very quickly with her head averted just in case anyone was watching from the upstairs window. She felt almost guilty about being in this street. Once safely out of sight however, she felt despondent. How on earth was she ever going to start having fun if she didn't have the confidence to do anything positive? It was depressing. If only Steve had seen her passing and called down. It wasn't the first time she'd walked home this way, always hoping she'd bump into him. She never had. Now, quickening her pace, she scowled aggressively at the pavement in front of her toes and felt her shoulders drop. Life was an absolute pain sometimes, she reflected.

When she arrived home, her mum was in the kitchen although the television was blaring from the lounge. Mrs Vaughan couldn't seem to stand silence these days. She always had the television or stereo on, as background noise, she said.

'Had a nice time, love?' she called, briskly buttering rolls and sliding slices of ham into them.

'Hm,' Rachel murmured, licking butter off the edge of a plate with her finger.

'Don't do that!' her mum said automatically and turned to the biscuit barrel.

'Why are you packing lunches now?' Rachel asked, suddenly aware of the activity going on around her.

'Because I've got two days temping down at Drayton. I won't have time to mess around in the morning. I won't be home until half five either, so remember your key and get yourself some tea. There's plenty of salad in the fridge.'

'Oh, well, could I go round to Sue's house, then?' Rachel asked as casually as possible, her mind racing through various plans.

Her mum stopped packing food and gave her a sharp look.

'You don't normally go round there – I didn't think you knew Sue very well.'

'Oh well, we've got a bit more friendly just lately.'

'Shall I phone her mum in a minute and see if it's OK for you to have tea with them tomorrow, then?'

'Don't be daft, Mum – she'll think you're being fussy. Anyway, it's only a suggestion. I might come straight home. It depends on how much homework I get.'

'Well, all right then, but be home at seven o'clock

definitely. I'm going out in the evening so I want to see you back here before I leave.'

Rachel looked up with interest.

'Where are you going?'

'To the theatre. There's a new play on which I've been wanting to see.'

'Who are you going with?'

Mrs Vaughan flushed ever so slightly and replied, too casually, 'John, from the bank.'

'Oh,' Rachel said, attempting, not very successfully, to disguise the disapproval in her voice. She had met John Wilson only once or twice but instinctively disliked him. He was ridiculously jovial and hearty. Her mother always laughed at his inane jokes but Rachel thought they were pathetic. He was an assistant bank manager, and the treasurer at church. Mrs Vaughan was always remarking on his clever head for figures, and he was giving her a lot of advice now that she was responsible for all her bills. Money had become increasingly important, so it seemed, since her father's departure. Now everything revolved around expense, and Rachel could sense that her mum was always anxious about their financial state.

Rachel wanted to ask if it had been John on the phone as she had been going out but she didn't want to pry.

'Have you put out your clothes for tomorrow?' her mum queried, breaking into Rachel's thoughts.

'I'll do it in a minute.'

'No, now! Come on, I want you up and out of the house early tomorrow. You can drop in to the news-agent's on your way to school and pay for the papers. I don't want them thinking we're getting behind with the payments. We owe for last week – the money's in the jar. Keep the receipt.'

'All right,' Rachel sighed, not in the mood for arguing,

even though it would make her late for registration.

She stopped pushing crumbs around the worktop and picked up her school shoes which her mum had polished.

'Night, Mum,' she said, waiting with up-tilted face for a kiss. Mrs Vaughan dropped a light kiss on the top of her head and turned back to her washing-up with a preoccupied air. The television was still blaring as Rachel trudged slowly up to bed.

4

The next morning was warm, and a light breeze eddied swirls of dust across the open playground of Oakwood High, Rachel's school. She stood in a corner of the yard near the fourth-year tutor rooms with the usual crowd which included Vanessa.

As lower formers they had been in a modern low building and in various huts grouped around the junior yard. Now however, they were in the sombre buildings of the original school, which formed a loose rectangle around Oakwood House, after which the school had been named.

The graceful white building housed the library, staff room, headmaster's study and the art rooms which doubled as sixth-form tutor bases. There was a wide spiral staircase with flagstone steps and a dark mahogany handrail. The old house had a peculiarly musty smell which Rachel always associated with her first day at the school and being lost in its maze-like corridors. It still felt threatening after four years of familiarity and use.

Art was first lesson for Rachel. She stopped off at the library to grab an illustrated book of flowers which she vainly hoped would pass for preparation to the still life lesson. Flicking through the pages she dashed up the wide staircase, muttering to herself. Consequently, she failed to notice Steve descending until they were almost face to face.

'Oh! Hi!' he said, sidestepping to avoid her.

'Sorry!' she returned briefly and then all at once recognised him. It was too late to put on a pretty, casual pose, or smile coyly or even to turn red with embarrassment.

'Oh, I didn't see you,' she said needlessly.

'In a hurry?' he asked.

'Sort of – I didn't quite finish my homework so I had to get to the library, and now I'll be late for the lesson.'

'Tut, tut!' he said in mock gravity. 'Not a good example to our fellow pupils is it!'

Rachel pulled a face. 'It's Mrs Pope next and she'll throw a fit if I turn up with nothing.'

'You couldn't make it last night, then?'

'Er, no!'

'Did it take longer than your mum thought?'

'What?' Rachel said blankly.

'Mowing the lawn – you were helping your mum, you said.'

'Oh that!' she exclaimed, rapidly catching up with the conversation.

'Yes it did – all evening in fact. I'm sorry – maybe another time,' she added, desperately hoping she wasn't sounding too pushy or too stupid. It occurred to her, simultaneously, that it would be impossible to spend all afternoon and evening cutting a lawn, unless you were using a pair of scissors. He must be thinking she was a complete idiot. But to her utter amazement he said, 'Yeah, why not – what about tonight then? Come round for coffee, then we can go out for a ride on the bike. The usual crowd will be there. We'll probably end up down at the beach.'

Rachel stood dumbfounded. She couldn't believe this

was happening to her. Steve Wilson had asked her out – just like that – and she hadn't even been thinking about him.

Steve broke into the ensuing silence with, 'Of course, if you're busy . . .' and she detected, with surprise, the note of uncertainty in his voice.

'No, I'd like that very much,' she stammered.

'Right, about seven then.'

'Right, fine.'

They were left in the awkward position of having no more to say yet being unable to finish the conversation. Almost simultaneously they spoke and then laughed.

'You'll be late,' Steve said.

'Oh yes. I must go. See you,' she blurted and fled up the remaining stairs. It was only later that she discovered that the cover of the illustrated flower book had been almost twisted away from the binding during those agonising, delicious moments.

The fact that Rachel had to find her seat in front of Mrs Pope's disapproving gaze and accept a reprimand on the vices of being late; that her inadequate preparation and total lack of concentration throughout the lesson were finally sufficient to provoke threats of detention, were all as nothing compared to the memories of the meeting. The rest of the day passed in a blur of excitement and dread, in about equal proportions. She spent most of Maths deciding what to wear and part of English making a list in the back of her exercise book of possible things she could talk about.

Walking home with Vanessa, Rachel could hardly wait to share her news. Vanessa was droning on about Maths homework and Rachel blatantly ignoring her until finally Vanessa said, 'What on earth's up with you? You're like a Cheshire cat!'

'Am I?' Rachel mused infuriatingly.

'All right, who is he?'

'What do you mean?' Rachel flashed, indignant at her own transparency.

'Well it's pretty obvious it's got to be a boy who's put you in this mood.'

'What mood?'

'Love!'

'I'm not in love!' Rachel exclaimed hotly, then with a grin said, 'Just interested.'

'Who then?' Vanessa challenged, feigning unconcern.

'Guess!' Rachel teased childishly.

'Oh good grief, how should I know? Um, Gary Smith?'

'Joke. Try again.'

'Mark Briggs?'

'He's foul. Come on – someone fantastic.'

' "Beauty is in the eye of the beholder" dear heart,' Vanessa quoted deftly.

Suddenly boring of the game and anxious to tell anyway, Rachel wrote his initials in the air.

'Oh,' said Vanessa flatly and her mood became suddenly gloomy.

'Oh, what?'

'Steven Wilson. OK. So it's him.'

'Is that all you've got to say?'

'What do you want me to say?'

'Is he fantastic or is he fantastic?' Rachel joked, trying to revive her own spirits.

'If you like that type,' Vanessa returned frankly.

'Oh, for goodness sake, Nessa, you're beginning to sound like Andy. What's wrong with Steve?'

'He's a loudmouth, a poser, he's rough – that'll do for starters.'

'That's just where you're wrong then.'

'You don't honestly think he's interested in you, for who and what you are!'

34

'Yes I do think he is. More to the point, I'm interested in him, his way of life. It's more exciting than . . .'

'Than what?'

'Than spending Friday evenings in a church hall playing table tennis and the best looking lad's spotty Graham or quote-me-a-text Andy.'

'So you'd prefer roaring round town on a pathetic bike, crude jokes, filthy magazines and a load of ignorant yobs.'

'Steve is not a yob!'

'Well, his mates aren't exactly your perfect gentlemen, are they?'

The deadlock ended in a silence which lasted for several minutes. Rachel was stubbornly determined not to give way. Vanessa, with less to lose, eventually said, 'Well, has he asked you out then?'

'I thought you weren't interested," Rachel snapped but then relenting a little she said, 'I'm seeing him this evening.'

When there was no reply she continued more gently, 'He's not like you think, Nessa. He's really nice – and I never thought he'd be interested in me.'

'Why not?' Vanessa demanded stoutly, her loyalty outweighing her disapproval.

'Because I'm boring, and ugly and stupid.'

'You're not boring, idiot – and you're one of the prettiest girls in our year, you toad!'

'You're just saying that.'

'Stop fishing for compliments. I didn't say you weren't stupid, actually, so you needn't be proud of the others!'

Rachel grinned and felt some of her former high spirits return.

'Why don't you come too?'

'Oh great!' Vanessa returned, heavily sarcastic.

'There's other people going. It's not just Steve and

me. You'd be welcome, honestly.'

'No thanks, I've got my homework to do.'

'So have I but you've got to get your priorities right, haven't you?' Rachel returned, half jokingly.

'I'm not going to have a row about your boyfriend. I've told you what I think of Steve's crowd and you won't convince me otherwise. I think you're getting yourself mixed up with a bad lot – I just hope you know what you're doing and won't regret it.'

'Sermon finished?'

'Yes.'

'Right then, I'll see you tomorrow – and let you have all the scandalous details, if you aren't afraid of having your pure ears tainted,' Rachel teased.

Vanessa attempted a smile but Rachel could tell she was perfectly serious.

'Look, Nessa, I know what you're thinking but you're wrong. I'm not about to go wild and freak out. I just want to have a bit of harmless fun.'

'I don't know whether Steve's lot *are* harmless.'

They had reached Vanessa's house by now. She stood with one hand on the gate and tried one final argument.

'Would they be the sort of people you could bring to church?'

'Don't be daft!' Rachel retorted. 'They wouldn't go to church.'

'That's not the point. Could you introduce them to your friends at church?'

'What does it matter?' Rachel parried.

'If you couldn't do that, then you're changing yourself to fit in with their image.'

'Maybe I like their image better,' Rachel said, more to herself than in answer to Vanessa's comment.

'Then I'm sorry for you – I like you as you are.'

'Oh, so tomorrow you won't like me?!'

'I didn't say that. Just don't let them give you a new identity.'

Rachel didn't answer. She scraped her foot along the gravel path, absorbed in her own thoughts. Then decisively, she flicked her hair out of her eyes.

'See you tomorrow?' she asked purposely.

'Yeah, of course,' Vanessa grunted, punching her roughly on the arm. Then she turned and walked quickly up to her front door.

As Rachel hurried home she felt so confused and ill at ease that she vaguely contemplated going back to Vanessa's and spending the evening with her. It would be the easier option, she thought, but then another stronger voice spoke. The chance of a lifetime, the boy you've been dreaming of, and now you're going to duck out? You must be mad, or pathetic. This is it. What you've been waiting for: real life, real excitement. Vanessa's warnings and doubts melted away. Of course she was going.

5

By the time Rachel arrived home she was breathless with excitement and nervousness. She fished her key out of her pocket and could hardly get it into the lock for her trembling fingers. Upstairs in her room, Rachel hurled her schoolbag against the wall and started peeling off her school uniform.

Next door in the bathroom, she started hot water gushing into the bath and then, wrapping a towel round her, she raced downstairs to the phone. Rachel dialled Sue's number carefully and then waited impatiently while the dialling tone bleeped. At last it was answered and Sue's voice was at the end of the line.

'Sue?'

'Yes.'

'It's Rachel.'

'Oh, yeah. You're coming tonight, aren't you?'

'Um, yes. I wondered . . . could I come round to your house before, in about an hour?'

'Sure. Any time you like. Come and have a bite to eat, then we'll go on to Steve's place and meet the others.'

'Oh, great. Thanks, Sue.'

'See you then.'

'Yeah. Bye.'

Rachel replaced the receiver and almost hugged herself with delight. Everything was going perfectly to plan. It would be much easier to arrive at Steve's with Sue than on her own. Sue hadn't sounded in the least bit surprised. Maybe Steve had spoken to her. It was perfect. She could leave a note for her mum to say she was having supper at Sue's and then be back before the theatre performance ended. No questions asked so no need for lies.

Soaking in the bath, Rachel felt a tiny prick of conscience about not being able to tell her mum what she was doing. Still, she reflected, there was no doubt about it. Her mother would be horrified about her going anywhere near a motorbike, so simply saying nothing was far easier. Anyway, she thought, justifying her actions, she wasn't doing anything wrong – just having a good time. That was worth a few white lies, surely.

Rachel had never been inside Sue's house and as she was led up to Sue's bedroom she was a bit shocked. There seemed to be people everywhere and Rachel didn't recognise any of them. There was a strong smell of cooking and the stair carpet was so worn that it looked greasy. From another room someone was shouting angrily but a loud thud suddenly ended the tirade.

They finally got inside Sue's room after a pile of dirty washing behind the door had been shoved aside.

'Right, park yourself somewhere,' Sue directed and darted out again, leaving Rachel to search in vain for a space to sit. Eventually she pushed some tatty school books and magazines to one side of the worktop and perched uncomfortably on one corner. She couldn't help but compare her own relatively neat room with this one. There were crumpled clothes strewn all over the bed and across the floor. Opened tubes of make-up and bottles of perfume decorated the dressing table while at least half of the mirror was plastered with pop group posters. Half-open drawers assumed a drunken appearance. They were too full of underwear and magazines to close properly so had been left at crazy angles, with their contents threatening to spill out at any moment.

Just then Sue knocked the door open with the edge of a plastic tray, edged in and then skilfully toed the door closed and placed the tray on the floor.

'Crikey, what a row!' she announced. 'We'll eat up here out of the way.'

'Are you sure your mum doesn't mind me being here?' Rachel asked,

'Don't think she knows you are. She wasn't listening when I told her.'

'Oh, Rachel said, rather nonplussed.

'It's OK. It's always a madhouse here. Dig in then,' said Sue, indicating the plates on the tray. Rachel eyed the egg and chips sliding on a pool of grease dubiously but she was hungry enough to plough in. It was cosy amidst the chaos of this household in a strange way. Her own mum would have laid out the best china and worried Sue to death with irrelevant questions about her home and family. Here, a rough hospitality was dealt out. You took it or left it and nobody worried. It was refreshing, sort of.

'So you're riding with Steve tonight,' Sue said between mouthfuls. It was a statement rather than an enquiry.

'Er, yes.' Rachel glanced at her nervously, trying to gauge her reaction but she could read nothing from Sue's indifferent expression.

'I'm with Jeff tonight,' Sue commented.

'Where do you usually go?' Rachel asked.

'Oh, down the far end of the prom, Monks Point. Gives you a good burn-up down past the dunes and no coppers to check on speed. Then we have a few coffees at the café there, bit of a laugh, you know the sort of thing.'

'What time do we get back?'

'Why – you on limits?'

'Sort of, I mean Mum likes me to be in by ten normally.'

'Crikey – things start warming up by then.'

'Don't you have to be in any time?'

Sue blinked and laughed. 'You've got to be joking! With the rumpus going on down there who's to notice anyway? I just make sure I belt up the stairs quick when I do get in. It's usually about eleven.'

Rachel felt her stomach sink as she sensed the situation getting out of hand. Her mum would be in soon after ten and if she wasn't in by then – it didn't bear thinking about. Again, Rachel contemplated bowing out before she got in too deep but again those voices in her head seemed to be prodding and coaxing her forward. Just once in her life she wanted to do something that wasn't quite safe. Vanessa had talked about paying for things. Well, she was certainly going to be paying for this, she decided ruefully. But the prospect of riding with Steve glowed in her imagination. More than that, the knowledge that she herself had chosen to do this and planned it made the evening special. To Sue it was nothing, a laugh at the most. To Rachel it represented a kind of independence and freedom she had hardly tasted before. It was too late to turn back now.

'Right, you fit?' Sue said, swinging her leather jacket over her shoulder.

'Yes, great,' Rachel managed.

'Away we go, then!'

They were meeting the others at Steve's house and as they waited at his front door, Rachel felt her palms go clammy. She immediately pushed them into her jeans pockets and made a mental note to ask to use the loo so she could wash them in cold water.

Then the door was open and Steve was framed in the doorway. He said hello to them both but smiled at Rachel. He looked different out of school clothes, older, and Rachel felt suddenly shy of him. She couldn't look him in the eye. Panic seized her as she sought desperately for some words to say. It was awful. How she wished she'd never come. And now they were heading up to his room where there was a hubbub of voices and music. It was like watching a movie of yourself – a silent movie – where all the dialogue came up on cards and the actors were ridiculously dramatic and artificial. Rachel positioned herself firmly behind Sue and prayed that she wouldn't be noticed by the others. Even Steve seemed horribly awkward and quiet now. All her well-prepared topics for conversation deserted her. It was so agonising that she felt angry, mostly at herself but also at Steve because he was just standing there, unable to help her.

As they trooped into Steve's room, everyone looked up and there was a momentary lull but, much to Rachel's relief, conversation rapidly picked up again. She only knew Sue really and although she tried to join in on her conversation, she felt more and more tongue-tied and self-conscious. Eventually she gave up listening and picked up the sleeve of an LP which someone was listening to. It wasn't one of her favourite groups but she read every printed word on it about three times before replacing it. When she looked up, Steve was sitting near her. Funnily enough, she felt more nervous of him than all the others in spite of the fact that he was trying hard now to make her feel at ease.

'Do you like that group?' he asked.

'Um, yes, quite, but I prefer . . .'

'Sorry, can't hear you with all this din,' he grinned

and moved a little closer. At that range she could smell his after-shave. Her mother would have made a face and called it overpowering. It was a rather raw, heady smell but Rachel liked it. It reminded her of the bathroom smell in the mornings after her dad had shaved. She'd missed it. It was reassuring.

Rachel started talking again, making what she felt were rather silly comments but Steve listened seriously and asked lots of questions, about her family and herself. She'd made up her mind that she wasn't going to lie about her friends, or about going to church – after all, they were a part of her life – but she wasn't going to start on about them if it wasn't natural to do so. When eventually she did mention the Bible classes she attended, Steve didn't smile or make a joke which was the usual reaction. He even seemed quite interested, but she was sure that was just out of politeness. Still, she felt the triumph of being able to tell Vanessa that he hadn't scoffed or criticised. Rachel began to relax. Steve was in the middle of describing a pop concert he'd been to up in Leeds when one of the girls, called Linda, suddenly cut across with, 'Terribly sorry to break up you two, but are we sitting here all night?'

Steve looked a bit nettled but he got to his feet and assumed control with calm assurance. His confidence was the thing that most attracted and impressed Rachel. The others looked to him for leadership but he wasn't domineering or aggressive.

'Right, Jeff, you go first with Sue, Linda you're with Phil. Rob's already gone so that just leaves Rachel with me.'

There was instant movement as the group filed out of the house and around to the narrow back alley where the bikes were lined up.

'Have you ridden before?' Steve asked.

'Yes,' Rachel lied and then compromised with, 'but it was ages ago.'

'Well, there's nothing to it. Lean with me when we go into the bends and make sure you keep your feet still. There's a bar behind to hold onto, until you get your balance. Here's your helmet. It's my sister's so it ought to fit you.'

'Thanks.' Rachel pulled on the helmet and struggled with the buckle under her chin in vain.

'Here, let's help you do it up,' Steve offered. He stooped to adjust the buckle for her and she could feel his warm fingers on her cheek for just a few seconds.

'OK?' he asked.

Rachel nodded and stood back while the bike was kick-started. Every inch of chrome glistened and winked in the red evening sunlight. It looked magnificent and powerful. The engine choked once or twice and then thundered into life. The noise echoed in the narrow alley and Rachel couldn't catch Steve's words any more, above the deafening roar. She saw him kick up the stand pedal and then gesture for her to climb on. The machine seemed massive now and Rachel couldn't tell which part of it she could safely trust to stand on. Very clumsily she clambered up, nearly getting her foot stuck in the back bar in the process.

'OK?' Steve shouted hoarsely over his shoulder.

'Yes,' she mouthed, and at that moment the bike shot forward in a lunging jerk. Rachel had been sitting upright with her hands lightly tucked under the bar behind her. The sudden forward impetus whipped her backwards with a stomach-churning jolt. Instinctively she grabbed Steve around the waist in a bear-hug and had to give up any hopes of appearing cool and unconcerned. Later, she reflected that maybe Steve had intended it to happen anyway.

6

At first it felt horribly precarious. As they braked for the town centre traffic lights they seemed to converge so quickly on the next car that Rachel closed her eyes and felt her hands clench into Steve's jacket.

'All right?' he said as the engine idled in the traffic queue.

'Fine,' Rachel returned brightly, wishing fervently that she could get off.

Then they were away again. This time Rachel braced herself for the initial lurch and, once they were rolling, managed to edge down the seat again and loosen her grip slightly. The first roundabout was horrific. Probably partly for her benefit, Steve threw the bike with alarming force into the bend. Rachel fought against her initial reaction to lean against the angle of the bike but had to close her eyes again to blot out the rush of ground which was coming up to meet them on their right hand side.

Then they were out on the main coast road. The traffic thinned. It seemed to Rachel that they were reaching incredible speeds but a glance at the milometer over Steve's shoulder showed that they were travelling at only forty miles per hour. She tried to look forward but the air stream caught her breath and she was forced into the lee of Steve's shoulder. Rachel could only look down or sideways. The rush of grey road below was a soft haze and green hedges whipped by like emerald candy floss. It was fantastic and more exhilarating than anything she'd ever experienced before. Rachel pushed her face into Steve's back and smelt the oily leather.

Her own jacket was hopelessly inadequate protection, even on this bright evening, and she was bitterly cold. Her fingers were white and she didn't think she could uncurl them now anyway. Rachel inched herself closer to Steve for warmth and felt suddenly safe next to him while the once familiar universe tore past them.

On the outskirts of Brintham, they caught up with Phil and Sue. Sue waved across at Rachel who just managed to disengage one hand to return a quick wave. There was a stiff breeze along the coast road which ripped through the ends of Rachel's hair and made her eyes sting. They accelerated away from Brintham's main centre and dimly Rachel made out the stubby cliffs of Monks Point. Rows of white and green beach huts slid in and out of focus to their left, while beneath them the centre road markings became a crazy continuous line and Rachel could taste the salt air on her lips. She wished they could just keep riding, now that she was used to the sensation. Rachel felt she understood the thrill of biking now. She could see what kept so many of the fifth-year boys slaving away at the local stores all hours of the weekend in an attempt to secure a deposit on the first bike.

Too soon, the coast road petered out and the cliffs loomed up, a natural barrier. They glided to a halt as Steve cut the engine prematurely and Rachel almost felt the impact of the silence which massed around them before either spoke. Rachel climbed down from the bike reluctantly, to feel her knees trembling beneath her.

Although she was standing quite still, she retained the impression of being flung through space. In the brisk sea breeze Rachel shuddered.

Steve took off his gloves and helmet and walked over to her. Rachel fiddled clumsily with the chin strap and finally found the buckle. She threaded a hand through her hair, wondering what kind of a state it was now in, but her excitement held, bubbling over her nervousness.

'That was fantastic!' she breathed.

'OK then?' He looked pleased.

'Brilliant!'

'That was nothing. You wait till we really get some speed up. We got snarled up in the traffic tonight. Here, let's take your helmet,' he said and as he reached out to receive it, brushed her fingers with his own.

'Hey you're frozen!'

'Oh no, just my hands,' Rachel said.

'You should have said. Look, put my coat on.'

'It's all right, honestly,' Rachel replied, but her teeth were starting to chatter.

Steve took off his coat. 'Put it on,' he ordered and she grinned at him, thankfully drawing the heavy, far too large coat around her.

Phil came over and offered them cigarettes from a grubby packet. Rachel shook her head but Steve took one, rather to her surprise. She'd never imagined that he might smoke. Not that it mattered of course, she said to herself, but still, she couldn't help wishing that he didn't.

Apart from a few more beach huts the only other building at this end of the esplanade was a small, shabby-looking café with gaudy shutters and grimy windows. They went in and took over two plastic-covered tables near the fruit machines. In a few minutes an aged, weary-looking waiter came over and took their orders for coffee.

Rachel smiled up at him when he shuffled back but he was oblivious to anything it seemed. At any rate, nothing could break through his sour expression. The cups were plonked down without ceremony, the brown liquid slopping into most of the saucers. Even the bowl of cubed sugar seemed to have absorbed some of the liquid, judging by the colour of the contents. Linda and Jeff were playing on the fruit machines, stabbing at the buttons and laughing loudly.

'Here, choose some music, Rachel,' Steve said, dropping some ten pence pieces in front of her.

Rachel jumped up, desperately trying to decide what sort of music the others would like. It took her ages just trying to work out how you selected the numbers and fed in the digits. Twice the ten pences clattered out of the reject slot because she'd forgotten to press the right button. Finally she chose two records from the LP at Steve's house and two more from the top ten, so at least Sue would like them. Again, she felt angry at herself. Why didn't she know how to work these machines and how to act in a place like this? It was all very well being in the top set for Art and French but where did that get you in a beach café at the rougher end of town?

Rachel had never been anywhere like this before and she wanted to absorb every detail. The overall impression was seedy. Everything was in bad taste, from the orange lino on the floor to the plastic daisies on the counter near the till. She almost laughed out loud at the prospect of her mum ever drinking coffee in a place like this. But she felt grown up sitting there with these apparently super-cool people. It was a very far cry from the youth club. These people were rough, loud and exciting to be with. Rachel didn't know whether she fitted in here or not, but she wanted to be part of it, part of the group. It felt good – and fun.

A bit later on someone produced some cards but since she didn't recognise the games Rachel opted to watch. She still felt shy with Steve but she saw that he tried very hard to involve her in conversation and seemed really anxious in case she was bored or not enjoying the evening. There wasn't much time for private conversation but she liked sitting close to him, watching him snap cards down, most of all feeling that she was with him, and all the others knew and accepted it.

Not being able to talk much to him gave Rachel a chance to watch the customers as they came and went, the old waiter as he shuffled around, and to feel the atmosphere of the place. It was all fascinating. The waiter had a habit of walking half-way across the floor and then scratching his ear before completing the journey to some table in a gloomy corner. His apron was tied up with various broken pieces of tape all knotted together and a greyish, limp dishcloth poked out of the pocket. He never actually spoke to any of his customers but a variety of gestures covered all essential communication.

Eventually the card game broke up. Jeff and Rob started playing darts and Steve and Rachel found themselves alone at the table.

'You OK then?' he said, casually.

'Fine, thanks.'

'You've been quiet.'

'Sorry.'

'You don't have to say sorry!' he laughed. 'I just thought you might be bored, or wishing you hadn't come.'

'Oh no. I've had a fantastic evening – really fun.'

'Good.'

Suddenly Rachel thought that maybe he wasn't enjoying being with her – that he had been bored all evening. The doubt grew into a certainty as minutes

passed by without either of them speaking and he sat
bending the corners of two cards between his thumb
nails. The silence grew until it was oppressive.

'Are you bored?' Rachel suddenly shot at him. 'I mean
would you prefer to play darts with the others?'

'No, I was enjoying just sitting here with you.'

'I'm not very interesting to talk to!' she laughed,
acutely self-conscious.

'Why not?'

'I never say anything!'

'Yes, you do. I'm glad you came tonight.'

'Are you?'

'Of course.'

'Why did you ask me?' she said, very seriously.

'Crikey, what a question! I like you.'

'Why?'

'Why what?'

'Why me? I'm not like, well, Linda or Sue for a start.'

'Thank goodness.'

'I mean I'm shy and quiet, and I've never ridden a
bike before or been in a place like this.'

'You said you had!'

'I lied,' she announced, bluntly.

They both laughed at that and their heads moved
closer together. It seemed easier to talk, now that they
were saying honest things to each other.

'Hey, why did you say "thank goodness" about me
not being like Linda or Sue? I thought you liked them.'

'I do. They're good fun but I wouldn't want to go out
with them. They're too loud for a start. A real show-
up.'

'I thought you were going out with Sue.'

'Yeah, well, she thought so. I couldn't be bothered to
argue the point. She just rode with me a couple of times,
that's all.'

'I was really surprised when you asked me out,' Rachel continued.

'Yeah, so was I.'

Rachel's eyes widened and Steve, suddenly aware of what he'd said, blushed as he fought for the right words, 'Er, I didn't mean it like that, I just meant . . .'

'Oh, that's OK!' Rachel said in mock indignation. They laughed again.

Steve looked at her, seriously, and Rachel felt a warm glow filter steadily into her cheeks.

'You're different,' he said.

'So are you,' Rachel replied softly.

It made her very happy that he was so different. They chatted on until the others came back. Jeff was bored and wanted to move, so they spilled out onto the pavement and drifted towards the parked bikes opposite. Rachel was just thinking that maybe she would be home in time when Jeff spotted something on the shore just below them and rushed off to check it out. The other lads went with him and soon Linda and Sue were hobbling across the pebbles too. Rachel had no option but to follow. Before she had caught them up, Rachel made out the dark form of a small rowing boat, left unmoored. There were always plenty of small boats dragged up on the beach near the quay, but Rachel had never seen one this far round the bay. There was just enough light to read the name, painted along the stern: *Lady Caroline*.

7

'Right ladies and gentlemen, step right up there for your moonlight cruise around the bay. Let's have yer money!' Phil mimicked the tourist-trapping boatmen who operated all through the summer season from the quay.

'Hey, why not?' Jeff joined in, and started to drag the boat down the beach. 'Give us a hand, Steve, it's heavy.'

Steve, who had been standing with his hands in his pockets, laughed softly and then bent down to take some of the weight.

'Lift, don't drag it!' he ordered. 'You'll tear the bottom.'

'Are there oars?' Sue said.

'Yeah, one's split but the other's OK.'

'What are you doing?' Rachel interrupted urgently.

'Crikey, she speaks!' Linda commented nastily.

'Trip round the bay,' Jeff said slowly, as if explaining to a small child. 'Just a laugh – it's low tide so we'll be safe enough if we just paddle around in the shallows.'

Rachel shook her head. 'That's not what I mean. It's not ours! The owner may be back tonight to moor her properly.'

'Not at this time of night,' Steve said, plainly perplexed by her reaction.

'We're not stealing it – just borrowing it,' Sue added.

By this time they were nearing the foamy ripples, and shingle had given way to wet sand. Rachel watched them struggle the boat into the light surf with a sinking feeling in her stomach. Sue took off her shoes and gingerly stepped aboard.

'Hang on! She's not afloat yet!' Jeff groaned.

'Well I'm not getting my feet wet,' Sue retorted and settled herself awkwardly in the bow. Linda followed just as a large wave swirled in and lifted the small craft up and out. Rachel stepped back and watched from the beach in mute silence. The lads were ankle-deep in cold water by now and started to clamber aboard. Steve gave one final push and then the *Lady Caroline* was launched and Rob was paddling madly, canoe-fashion with one oar. The girls were screaming and clinging onto the sides convulsed with laughter as Jeff flung himself headfirst into the boat.

'Come on, Steve, you'll get soaked!' Linda cried, waving frantically.

'There's no more room – go on, we'll watch,' Steve called back and then turned to where Rachel was standing. The laughter and screams from the boat became indistinct as the *Lady Caroline* bobbed clumsily out into the bay. Rachel, horrified and angry, turned back towards the road, trying to walk quickly despite the shifting shingle which gave way beneath every step.

'Hey, Rachel!' Steve called. 'Wait for me. Hang on!' he shouted, catching her arm. 'What's wrong for Christ's sake?'

'Don't!' she cried, shrugging him off.

'Don't what?'

'Just don't *say* that!'

Steve stepped away, as if stung. He looked hurt and bewildered.

'I don't understand,' he said. 'Why are you mad?'

She looked at him, her mouth trembling.

'It's not right. They shouldn't have taken the boat – and you helped them!'

'It's not dangerous. They're only in about six foot of water.'

'That's not the point! Oh, for goodness' sake, don't you understand? It's somebody else's property. You might damage it, they might come back. It's just stupid and it's not right.'

'You're afraid of getting in trouble,' he said gently.

'Yes I am,' she flared 'but more than that . . . we've got no right to behave like this, like a group of yobs . . .' Rachel couldn't remember where she'd heard that phrase today but it struck her as sounding strangely familiar.

'I'm sorry, I didn't realise.'

Rachel bit her lip and remained silent.

'Is that what you think I am?' Steve asked and the hurt look on his face shocked her. She hadn't realised that her opinion of him might actually matter. Slowly, Rachel felt her anger subside. It hadn't been his idea, after all. And he was here with her because he hadn't wanted to leave her on her own.

'No, I don't think that,' she stammered.

'Look, do you want me to call them back? I will if you like. Will you wait here for me?'

'Yes,' she said softly, relief flooding through her.

He smiled, sure of himself again. Suddenly he took hold of her hand and pressed it quickly in both of his. Then he was gone and in the dark she heard the thud and scrunch of stones as he ran across the beach. Rachel stood still, rubbing the hand Steve had touched against her cheek.

It had grown dark suddenly and Rachel could see lights up on the road. She wondered if anyone up there had seen them. Then, just as she was beginning to wonder how far away Steve was, she saw the flash of a torch eyeing its way slowly down the beach, barely a hundred yards away. Rachel felt her stomach turn over, sickeningly. Whoever it was would find them down there with the boat. It might even be the owner. Who else would be down here in the pitch black? He'd find her – he'd get the police! Rachel started running and sliding down to the shore, her heart hammering in panic.

'Oh God, please don't let it be the owner. Please let us get home. I'll never do anything like this again. I'm sorry . . .' she found herself stammering in desperate sentences.

Crashing onto the sand she caught sight of Steve and the others noisily disembarking and hauling the boat up out of the water.

'Steve!' she cried 'Look!'

The others followed her gaze and the laughter immediately subsided.

'That's all we need!' said Jeff. 'It's time we were scarce. We'll have to dump it over there. Come on, let's move.'

The three lads started up the beach, stumbling and swearing while Linda and Sue dragged the oars behind them, scraping them noisily over the stones.

'Hurry, please hurry,' Rachel breathed, almost crying now.

She glanced over her shoulder and saw the inevitable advance of the bobbing light. She calculated the distance between them almost clinically and then started walking in a straight line towards the light. There was no way the others could drop the boat in time unless she could stop whoever it was with the lamp.

Quite calmly, Rachel climbed diagonally across the beach. When she could discern the outline of a figure she stopped and waited until the torchlight fell across her path. In its yellow glow she made out the features of an old man. He had a pipe in the corner of his mouth which sent up great billows of smoke. A soft, tattered cap concealed his eyes.

'Oh, hello!' she said, as if startled to have met him.

'Evening, lass,' the man replied.

'Have you got the time, please?' It was the first thing she could think of to prevent him from passing straight on with his heavy, rolling stride.

'Past your bedtime I'd say,' he chuckled gruffly and then laboriously rolled up the sleeve of his jumper to find his watch. He turned around to shine the torch and as he did so, a half-moon glimmered out from behind the clouds, illuminating them both.

'Quarter to ten, love. What are you doing down on the beach? It's not the place for a lass, this time o'night. You don't know who you might meet.'

Rachel smiled to herself at these ironic words. 'I'm with my friends. They're up on the road but I came down to look at the water for a minute.'

'I'm surprised you didn't trip over my boat, then. She's just over there. Had to leave her unmoored and uncovered, but I've been working on her – getting a bit of new paint and varnish on, like.'

Rachel felt herself tighten. So this was the owner. 'No, I didn't see it,' she said slowly.

'That's odd, then,' he said. 'Still I dare say you'd miss her without a torch.'

'I thought all the boats were up at the quay.'

'Aye, so they are – and mine most of the time – but I decided to bring her up this end, out of the way, while I worked on her. It's a surprise see – for the wife. I don't want the missus to see her till she's finished, next week. It's her birthday, see. I've done the old boat up special, like. She thought I was out fishing today, but I was working on her here. Paint'll be dry now so I've come down to cover 'er up with a tarpaulin.'

'Oh, that's nice,' Rachel said in a small, hollow voice.

'Now lass, let's see you back up on the road.'

'It's all right, I can manage.'

'But it's dark, lass.'

'No, the moon's out again. I can see quite plainly.'

'Well, I'll stand and watch you up then,' the old man insisted.

'Thanks. Goodnight,' Rachel managed.

'Goodnight, lass.'

Rachel turned away, too shaken and scared to think any further than the end of her trek up the shingle. She hardly cared whether the others had got the boat back up the beach now. As she dragged the last few steps, she turned back to see the torch waving at her down on the shore. Silhouetted against the lighter sky, she waved back and then heard the rev of bike engines beside her.

'You're OK, girl.' Jeff said. 'That was close though! Thought the old codger'd see us for a minute there!'

'Yeah, thanks Rachel,' Linda murmured, albeit grudgingly.

Steve handed Rachel her helmet with a searching look and then he grinned. 'Talk about cool!'

Rachel managed a weak smile before she climbed onto the bike. Moments later they were off. The wind rushing across her cheeks made them cool but her heart still thumped wildly and she couldn't blot out the image of the kind old man. What would he think when he found the boat? Would he assume she was connected? Would he know they'd taken her out? Yes, he was bound to. Then the real horror struck her – had they damaged her, scraped the new, raw paint? Why had he had to tell her all about his wife – she didn't even know his name. Why did old people tell you so much about themselves – make you know what you didn't want to know? They'd got away with it, but what had they done? The worst thing was that she'd played a key part in it. And the others thought she was so cool, so clever! It was laughable, really incredibly funny. Only she didn't feel much like laughing. Rachel barely noticed the ride home. She held on tightly to Steve and tried to push out the thoughts which raced round her mind. It was all spoilt though. That was the one feeling which crowded out every other.

Steve dropped Rachel off at her house at half past ten. Incredibly, her mother wasn't in. Rachel had practically resigned herself to a full confession and the consequent row, but when it didn't happen that, too, added to her guilt. They hardly spoke as Steve walked her up to her front door. Rachel was too preoccupied to pay him much attention. She didn't know what she felt about him any more. Part of her hated him, because she was feeling so wretchedly guilty and, of course, it was his fault. Well, he was to blame for what had happened, wasn't he?

'Hey, look. I'm sorry about tonight . . .' he began awkwardly as they stood at Rachel's front door.

'I've got to go,' she interrupted harshly. 'Thanks for bringing me home. Goodbye,' she added stiffly, and turned on her heel, leaving him there. Rachel felt angry tears of frustration start to flow as she flung the curtains together in the lounge. Automatically, like a practised criminal, she punched cushions to suggest an evening spent in front of the TV, even putting a mug into the washing up bowl as if she'd drunk from it. She was just climbing into bed as she heard her mother turn the key in the lock. If only, she thought, pressing her hands to her temples, her mum had been in, ranted and raved, demanded an explanation. It would have been horrible but at least then her mum would have known about it, and Rachel wouldn't now feel so wretched. Tomorrow she would have to lie to her mum about where she'd been, and who knew what new terrors the next day might bring? Was there any way the old man could trace them? She hadn't actually done anything, but he'd seen her and spoken to her. And he would know that she had purposely deceived him. That was the worst part of all. It was horrible in every way. When sleep eventually came, Rachel dreamt of sailing all alone in a boat which was taking in water as fast as she could bale it out.

8

The next morning Vanessa searched Rachel out in the school yard before first bell. It was a windy day, threatening rain and the open playground was bleaker than usual. Vanessa was curious in spite of herself but she waited patiently for at least two minutes before beginning her enthusiastic interrogation.

'Well, how'd it go, then?' she began.

'OK.' Rachel couldn't meet Vanessa's eyes.

'Are you seeing him again?'

'Maybe.'

'What's that supposed to mean?'

'What I said!' Rachel snapped.

'Crikey, Rachel, you either like him or you don't.'

'I do.'

'So what's the problem?'

Rachel shrugged her shoulders and stared out across the football field. Finally she glanced back to Vanessa and murmured, 'Something happened last night . . .'

Vanessa's mouth fell open in horror.

'Not what you're thinking, idiot.'

'I wasn't thinking anything,' Vanessa spluttered out in confusion. Rachel grinned wryly.

'Jeff and Rob, the others – they take a bit of getting

used to.'

'Well, I told you, didn't I?' Vanessa returned smugly. She was actually rather jealous that Rachel seemed to be deserting her for new friends. She was too good a friend to wish Rachel any unhappiness but she still hoped Rachel would drop them.

Rachel contemplated telling her all about the evening and the old man's boat but she decided against it. She knew how her friend would react, and that she deserved the criticism, but not just now. Anyway, maybe it could all be forgotten. First bell pealed out and there was a general surge towards the corridor entrances. The moment of confession was thankfully past. Last night Rachel had ached to share her problem. Now, covering it up and keeping it hidden seemed to be the most vital thing. She hoped she wouldn't bump into any of the group, especially Steve, that day.

As it turned out, it was very far from a normal day. For a start, odd twinges of fear and unease dogged her continually, dampening her appetite at lunch time and sapping her concentration. Lessons dragged on interminably and the final bell brought little relief. Steve was waiting for her outside her tutor room at twenty to four. Vanessa sniffed meaningfully and left Rachel to talk to him alone.

'I wanted to see you,' Steve began.

'Oh yes?' Rachel rummaged around in her school bag so she could avoid his eyes. She felt embarrassed by him.

'Can I walk you home?'

'No, thanks. I always walk with Vanessa,' she returned primly.

'Oh, I see.'

There was an awkward silence.

'Look, about last night . . .' he continued.

'I don't want to talk about it,' Rachel interrupted

sharply.

'I'm sorry, I thought you might be worried still, that's all,' he said stiffly.

'There's nothing to say. I'm trying to forget it, thank you.'

'Oh, well, if that's what you want . . .'

'Yes, that's what I want.' Rachel started to move away but to her irritation, he followed, though maintaining their formal distance.

'Will I see you again some time, then?' he asked, too casually.

'I don't know,' Rachel replied in a low tone.

'I see.'

They came to a halt but only for a moment. Steve looked very pale and Rachel almost opened her mouth to speak but at that moment, without saying goodbye, he moved abruptly away down the stairs, leaving her alone in the deserted corridor. It was one of the most miserable moments in Rachel's life. She'd been horrible to him. The truth was that she felt bad and so she had wanted to hurt him too. She didn't know who was to blame any more. Perhaps Vanessa had been right and Rachel just didn't belong with Steve and his crowd. She'd behaved like a spoilt, silly child and now she couldn't work out what was the real problem any more; whether it was the incident with the boat or her reaction to it. She couldn't forgive Steve for the way she was now feeling – that was the simple, ridiculous fact. But you're just as much to blame as him, Rachel thought. More, in fact, because you knew it was wrong from the start; the others didn't see it that way. Rachel could honestly believe that Steve hadn't seen anything wrong in using the boat. But she wanted him to pay for her guilt. The hollow, sick feeling in her stomach remained.

Shaking herself slightly, Rachel moved down the

corridor. She hadn't the heart to catch Vanessa up and suffer a further inquisition, so she trailed home alone, hoping for a quiet, uneventful evening. Rachel needed some time to get her thoughts sorted out. Ironically, it was when she was at home with her mother that the full force of the previous evening's events descended.

They had just finished eating and her mother was browsing through the local evening newspaper when a small item caught her eye.

'Oh, what a shame. Youngsters these days, honestly!' she exclaimed.

'Hm, what?' Rachel murmured, engrossed in a cartoon on the television.

' "Joyride in the bay spoils birthday surprise" ' her Mum quoted. 'Dear me, let's hope they catch them. Oh 'Fashion Show at the Town Hall'', she continued, with more enthusiasm. 'That might be worth going to.'

While her mum prattled on, choosing various snippets to read aloud, Rachel, sick with terror, gazed at the ridiculous antics of her favourite cartoon characters with furious attention. At last her mother pushed aside the paper and rose to take out their tea trays. As soon as she had gone, Rachel fell on the paper and rattled through the pages, her eyes scanning the headlines like radar. She found it, tucked between a motoring fine and the fashion show advertisement. It was barely ten lines long, giving the name of the boat, *Lady Caroline*, the owner, Mr Patrick Kennedy, and a description of the damage which had led to Mr Kennedy informing the police. The reporter played on the birthday aspect but there was nothing to suggest that the police had any clue as to who had caused the damage. It was simply supposed that it had been the work of teenagers. It wasn't as bad as it could have been. Maybe it would all blow over in a day or two, Rachel thought, wildly, but the feeling of panic wouldn't be quieted.

Rachel was sure she would go mad as she struggled to behave normally through a seemingly endless evening. She smiled grimly to herself at the memory of her mother's words – 'Let's hope they catch them'. I'll bet you wouldn't like it if they did, Rachel thought.

Rachel hadn't expected Steve to speak to her the next day at school, far less seek her out in the morning before registration but he spotted her with Vanessa and hurried over.

'Can I speak to you?' he said quietly and Rachel was so surprised that she let him pull her gently away from her group around the corner of the dining room.

'Well?' she said. The embarrassment she felt at not knowing how to express her conflicting feelings towards him made her voice sound cold.

'Bad news, I'm afraid.'

'Go on.'

'Did you see the paper last night?'

Rachel felt sick again. 'Yes.'

'The old bloke went to the police.'

'Yes, but he doesn't have our names or anything. I mean, he won't find out it was us, will he?' Rachel was shocked to find herself gabbling away and even more so when she recognised the self-interest in her words. The old man's problems were his now. She was only concerned with keeping out of it, not being found out. Even Steve looked a bit taken aback by her obvious panic.

'Well, I don't know. Trouble is, one of the lads dropped his wallet on the beach, probably near the boat. It hasn't got his name in, but it did have the last school disco ticket in, and some telephone numbers. And then of course, the old man can give a pretty good description of you.'

'Me!'

'Yeah, and then there's Jeff's telephone number.'

'We're going to be found out!' Rachel said, in horror, almost to herself. Then, realising the full implications of what that would mean: the shame, the awful scene with her mum, then her dad, Vanessa, Andy . . . 'It's all your fault!' she screamed at Steve. 'My mum'll kill me. Oh, why did I go with you lot? They told me about you! Oh. . . just leave me alone. I hate you!' The last words were almost spat out, in a moment of frustration and terror and Rachel regretted them the moment they were spoken. Steve stood quite still, accepting it all and then walked away without a word.

Vanessa, who had watched the scene from a distance, was at her side almost immediately.

'What was that all about?'

'Don't ask!' Rachel flashed, then grabbing Vanessa's arm she dragged her in the direction of their tutor room.

'Please just stay with me, Nessa. Don't say a word – just stay with me.'

The notice came round during second period, which was earlier than Rachel had anticipated. Their teacher, Mr Hall, read out the message irritably, because he'd been in the middle of a lengthy explanation about photosynthesis.

'All fourth and fifth years assemble in the hall at break time, promptly.' There was a groan and then a medley of curious whispers rippled around the lab.

'That'll do! Back to your notes, please.'

Vanessa gave Rachel a searching look but she remained silent. It was like being in a dream. When you were waiting outside the dentist's room, there was that moment when your name was called and you just walked forward to meet your fate even though you actually wanted to run. It was like going on to automatic pilot.

That was how she felt now. A kind of heady feeling swept over her. They were going to be accused, in front of the rest of the school and there wasn't a thing to be done about it. Well then, let it happen. She wouldn't deny it, or say it wasn't her fault. They could do what they liked. She was too tired and strung up about the whole thing to take much more. It would be almost a relief to have it out in the open.

It was strange lining up in the hall with the rest of her form and sensing the atmosphere of excitement and relish. Everyone loved trouble, when they weren't involved. Rachel could even see Sue and Linda opposite her in the hall. They hadn't spotted her yet, but they looked pale and seemed to be trying to attract someone's attention. Rachel followed their gaze, squinting to see who they were looking for but there were too many taller heads in the way.

The deputy head barked for silence and the buzz of voices dropped away. Then the head marched imperiously down the centre aisle and with him was the school liaison policeman. Rachel's heart gave an erratic thud and she felt the perspiration break out on her palms. She hadn't bargained for the police being here, not on school premises. Just what had they done? Was it really so very serious?

'You are probably wondering why I have called this assembly, during your own break time,' the head began in his favourite rhetorical style. 'Well, since most of my morning has been occupied by the matters I shall shortly relate, I felt it right that you too should suffer the inconvenience of having your free time wasted.' He paused for effect. Rachel eyed him cynically. Why didn't he get on with it? For one ridiculous moment she thought that maybe she was wrong – maybe this wasn't going to be about the boat at all. But his next words dispelled any further doubt. 'I was shocked to read an article in last night's paper entitled "Joyride in bay" which some of you may have seen . . . Now I am deeply distressed to learn that pupils from this school were responsible; indeed somebody standing before me.' The headmaster's eyes seemed to be everywhere, trying to root out the culprits. During the ensuing minutes Rachel caught only fragments of the lecture which the head delivered; 'flagrant stupidity,' 'reckless,' 'irresponsible,' 'criminal,' 'shameful' were some of the snatches which caught her attention. Still Rachel couldn't spot Steve's head among the sea of faces around her. She wondered how he was reacting to all this.

Finally the head rumbled to the end of this oration and there was a tense moment of silence. Rachel looked up and saw Vanessa eyeing her in a puzzled way.

'I want the person, probably persons, responsible to come forward . . . now,' demanded the head. 'I need not remind you of the severe light in which I will view any pupil who refuses to own up to the stupid but potentially dangerous crime which I have described. However, I will respect a speedy confession and think slightly more highly of the boys or girls concerned if they do not keep us waiting here any longer.'

Rachel stood, swaying slightly, waiting for her legs to take a first step. This was it – time to own up. But she didn't want to be the first. As soon as Linda or Sue moved, she would too. A minute ticked by and the headmaster coughed ominously. Somebody tittered nervously until the deputy head fixed a steely gaze on them.

Rachel was just wondering what sort of effect might be caused if she suddenly fainted or was sick over the floor when a movement behind caught her attention. A single figure walked towards the centre aisle and a space in the lines of bodies opened out before him. It was

Steve. Simultaneously, from another line of bodies, Jeff struggled out into the centre walkway. Rachel tried to look for Linda and Sue but she couldn't locate them. Steve was parallel with her form line now. She made an involuntary movement towards him but at that precise moment his eyes met hers and he shook his head. Rachel caught her breath, and almost moved again but he smiled at her, just a brief flicker of recognition, but she understood and remained where she was. Her eyes followed them as they approached the rostrum. Nobody spoke and the atmosphere was vaguely heroic.

The head drew himself up, and with a hand on each of the boy's shoulders whisked them away, out of the side doors. The policeman, looking redundant, followed at a more leisurely pace, a rather bored expression on his face. Conversation flared up and nobody bothered to stop it. There were still ten minutes of break remaining.

Vanessa had watched it all. She saw, and knew, but for once remained wisely silent. They walked slowly to the girls' cloakrooms where Rachel burst into tears and Vanessa was too busy handing out tissues to have time to offer any advice, or recrimination. Rumour and gossip ricochetted around for the rest of the day but the two friends stayed out of the conversations. However, Rachel couldn't help overhearing details and was hurt to learn of the boys' possible suspension from school, of parents being called in and possible damages to pay. They were consequences which she should have been sharing, but Steve and Jeff had chosen to take them. Most painful of all was the memory of how nasty she had been to Steve – yet he'd taken the blame for her. Her own guilt certainly hadn't been sufficient to persuade her to make a sacrifice for the others. What a turn of the tables!

9

'Well, that's that, isn't it? I mean, you won't be seeing him again, will you!' Vanessa said decidedly, as they walked briskly through the town centre later that day.

'Why not?' Rachel returned defensively.

'For goodness' sake, Rachel. You're the one who said you hated him for getting you into the mess. It's obvious – you now tell him where to go.'

'After what he's done for me?'

'That was the least he could do, considering it was his fault. So say thanks, but no thanks.'

'It was no more his fault than mine.'

'They're *his* friends. You surely don't want anything more to do with that lot? Haven't you learnt your lesson yet?'

'I think things could be different in the future.'

'How?'

'Next time I'll know what to do. I won't have anything to do with them if they're planning anything stupid.'

'You may not be able to help it. Looking on and not doing anything is just as bad as doing the thing in the first place.'

Rachel fell moodily silent.

'I still like him,' she confessed.

'I know,' Vanessa said softly. 'I can understand that, but is it worth it? He's not good for you.'

'Why not?'

'You're doing things out of character: changing, giving up the beliefs you had. You know that's wrong.'

'I only know I like him.'

'But what about church, your friends there? What's happened to your relationship with God?' she ended softly. 'Aren't you rejecting all that for Steve?'

It was true. The panic of being found out had gone but she was still in a turmoil inside. She couldn't think about God at all – it was as if a huge barrier had gone up between them. Rachel didn't think she would ever be able to sit in church comfortably again. All the lies, deceit, wrong thoughts and actions spun round in her brain. What was that hymn her Mum liked? *'Dear Lord and Father of mankind, forgive our foolish ways!'* and that line, *'Drop thy still dews of quietness.'*

If only she could talk to God personally and ask for forgiveness. But to be forgiven you had to repent – to never want to sin again – and yet she wanted to go out with Steve again. Was that just putting herself in the way of temptation again? Did it mean she wanted her own way more than loving God? Tears filled her eyes. No, that wasn't true. She did love God underneath everything. How she longed for the peace and safety of the church right now; for those eyes of Christ in the window knowing and loving her – not being hurt by her waywardness and rejection; the people who were caring and honest, who lived Christ's way and were prepared to stand out from the crowd. That took courage – more courage than riding fast bikes and stealing boats. She would be giving up all that for a crowd of people she didn't fit in with and didn't respect and a boy who didn't understand her desire to have a real relationship with God.

'Oh, Nessa, what am I going to do?'

Vanessa put an arm round her roughly but with real affection. 'Shall we pray about it?' Rachel nodded. 'You pray please.'

They sat down and held hands. Vanessa's words were clumsy and halting at first but gaining confidence, she continued, 'Father, you know what's happened today and how sorry Rachel is about Mr Kennedy. Please forgive her and show her what to do next. We both want to have a real relationship with you, God, so help us to listen to what you're saying and when we read the Bible, help us to understand it. Give Rachel your peace now. Amen.'

Rachel squeezed her friend's hand gratefully. She was still worried inside but somehow her mind seemed clearer.

'I think you ought to tell someone, I mean a grown-up. I wish you'd speak to Paul or Liz. They'd know what to do.'

'Maybe.'

'Look, I'll pray about you and Steve.'

'Thanks, Nessa – you're a mate. Do you think I'm really awful? You haven't said 'I told you so' yet.'

'All right, I told you so.'

They laughed.

'I hope I'm as much help one day,' Rachel said.

'God will be, whatever we are. It's him you've got to thank.'

'I know.'

Over the next few days, Rachel learned that, in fact, neither boys had been suspended but their parents had had to visit Mr Grant the headmaster to give assurances about future behaviour. On top of that there had been damages to pay but the police, having given a warning, took no more action.

Jeff's father had paid his son's share of the cost and expected Jeff to pay him back. Steve, on the other hand, had agreed to work off his debt by spending two hours down at the docks under Mr Kennedy's supervision, three days a week after school. Rob was paying his share through Jeff. Already in trouble with the police, Rob's name, together with the names of the three girls, had been kept secret. Mr Grant suspected, but as he had no proof and had the school's reputation to consider, prudently settled for two victims only. Whether Mr Kennedy had linked Rachel to the crime or not, he was apparently satisfied that justice had been done and withdrew charges. Within a very few days it was stale news around school and hardly merited a mention except among the first formers who continued to embroider the story in each retelling of it.

Rachel was at first anxious to see Steve but he was never in the usual places and, above a couple of glimpses, she did not see him for over a week. By that time she had convinced herself that he really wasn't interested in her any more and eventually she started to avoid him too. Her own sense of guilt, however, would not go away. With each day she felt more troubled by her part in the disastrous evening. Not being found out or made to pay had ironically made it worse. She thought about the series of Bible classes Paul had led on forgiveness and suddenly knew what it felt like to remain unforgiven. She knew that God forgave her but sensed that he wanted her to do something about it. Perhaps it was her fault, but she couldn't accept God's forgiveness until that 'something' had been done.

Who could she turn to? There seemed to be no one

whom Rachel could talk to who wouldn't immediately be shocked and horrified. But then she thought of Paul and Liz. They were far enough outside of the situation to be objective and she trusted them. Yes, she *could* talk to them.

'I'll give you a lift if you're ready to leave now.'

'Where are you going, then?' asked Rachel curiously as she watched her Mum brushing her hair with short strokes of the brush.

'I'm seeing John – just for coffee. I've got some accounts I want him to look over,' Mrs Vaughan replied casually.

'Oh.'

'Well, do you want a lift, or not?'

'Yes, please, I'll get my coat.'

'Is there a special meeting tonight then, for the young people's group?' Mrs Vaughan asked, as they reached the edge of their housing estate.

'Oh no, just a couple of us are going round to Paul and Liz for coffee,' Rachel replied, hoping it sounded plausible.

'I see. I thought you might have signed up for the baptism classes. They're due to begin soon, aren't they?'

'Are they?'

'I thought so.'

Mrs Vaughan concentrated on overtaking a car and then tried again.

'Had you thought of joining the class? It doesn't commit you to anything, if you don't feel ready.'

It was the first time for days that Rachel's mum had started a real conversation. She had seemed tired and preoccupied over the last week. Rachel couldn't tell her that there now seemed a hundred reasons why she couldn't contemplate baptism.

'I might chat to Paul about it tonight,' Rachel said.

'Yes, do that.' Mrs Vaughan fell silent again, but she looked pleased. Rachel noticed that she was wearing a new jumper and had put on some of her favourite perfume. The scent wafted under Rachel's nose from time to time. It made her think of the meeting with John.

'Do you like John?' Rachel asked suddenly, not even attempting to be tactful, because she simply wanted to know.

Mrs Vaughan looked uncomfortable but she was determined to be honest.

'I am fond of him, yes.'

To say Rachel was pleased would have been a lie. It occurred to her that her own secretive behaviour recently had somehow driven her and her mother apart. Nowadays, they didn't talk about anything very much. Had she been unfair and prejudiced about John? So many things which had once been clear now seemed hazy and confusing. Perhaps she'd been wrong about him too.

'Rachel, love, please remember that you are the most important person in my life. I wouldn't do anything to hurt you,' Mrs Vaughan said.

'Oh, Mum!' Rachel covered her mum's hand on the steering wheel with her own for a moment. 'I don't really know John. I haven't bothered, but if he makes you happy, I'll try to like him too,' she poured out.

'Silly girl,' her Mum replied fondly. 'It's not that serious yet. Anyway there's lots to think of, and a lot of praying for us both to do. It may not be right and I don't want to make any more people unhappy.'

It was the first time that Mrs Vaughan had ever hinted that the breakdown of her marriage might have been partly her fault.

'But Dad left you, Mum. It wasn't your fault,' Rachel said, struggling to make some sense out of the situation.

Mrs Vaughan stopped the car outside Paul's house and breathed deeply before turning to face her daughter.

'It's never just one person's fault, love. It took me a long time to see that, but do you know, your dad leaving threw me back on God and sent me back to the Bible. It was all I had left to turn to for comfort. At first I rejected what I was reading but, well, that bit in Corinthians on love really hit me. "Love never finds fault", it says, but I can't remember the last time I encouraged your dad. I was too bitter and angry with him. Eventually I began to realise that I had driven him away, just as surely as if I'd asked him to leave. It's too late in a way, but I'm not going to forget that lesson.'

There were tears in Rachel's eyes as she leant against her mum. Why hadn't they spoken before? So Mrs Vaughan was wrestling with her problems as well. Rachel felt closer to her mum than she had done for many months.

'And that's one reason why I want you to think about baptism and your relationship with God very carefully,' Mrs Vaughan continued. 'It's so easy just to let things ride and never take God seriously. I didn't for years and I've missed out on so much because of that. I know you're growing up and things like boy-friends, clothes, jobs and exams all seem so important – the *most* important things in fact – but they're not. I want you to have all those things too, but I'd rather you had a strong faith and a relationship with God. I'd know then that you had a solid basis for your life, even when circumstances are difficult or people let you down.'

Rachel had never heard her mum speak like this before. She wanted to tell her that it was all right, that she understood. She had spent so many hours recently thinking about Steve and new clothes and only the odd minute with God, usually when she wanted something! Strange how the other things became so attractive and powerful.

'I do know what you mean, Mum,' Rachel said.

'You'll be late,' Mrs Vaughan whispered. 'We'll chat when you get home.'

Rachel nodded happily and then slid out of the car. Before she slammed the door she cried out, 'Have a lovely time,' and she meant it.

Her mum smiled and waved.

10

Rachel approached the front door apprehensively. She didn't even know for certain that Paul or his wife would be in, but moments after ringing the bell she saw a figure take shape behind the frosted glass and then Paul was smiling down at her.

'Rachel, how nice! Come on in.'

The small hallway was crammed with boxes, piles of newspapers and a battered upright piano which didn't fit in any of the living rooms so had been relegated to the space under the stairs.

'Coffee?' Liz shouted from the kitchen. She was stirring the contents of a saucepan with one hand and cuddling a ginger cat under her other arm.

'Please,' Rachel said gratefully. It struck her once again that in this household, busy as it was, you always felt that your arrival had been almost expected. It was never necessary to apologise for interrupting anything.

Paul took Rachel's coat and flung it over the bannister and then showed her into the living room. Liz joined them with mugs of coffee and a large biscuit tin.

Rachel had always known that actually coming out with any sort of confession would be far too embarrassing. If the conversation just happened it would be

OK but otherwise she'd go away again. Ostensibly she was there to talk about the baptism classes and she persevered with her questions for a long time.

When Paul had outlined the basic arrangements and Rachel had nothing else to ask, she had almost decided that she wouldn't mention the other matter when Paul, very gently, said, 'Was there any other particular reason why you wanted to talk about the classes?'

It was the perfect opportunity. She was surprised at how easily Paul had guessed that there was something else on her mind. Rachel cleared her throat and then said quickly, 'The other day, I got into a bit of trouble – or at least some friends of mine did.'

'Go on,' Paul said and smiled.

'Do you want me to go, Rachel?' Liz offered.

'No, please stay, Liz.'

The whole story came out and neither Paul nor Liz interrupted until Rachel had finished.

'The main thing is that I feel so guilty about Mr Kennedy and his wife. I was just as much at fault and I didn't even take a part of the blame. Then I feel awful about the way I spoke to Steve – and I still like him even though I shouldn't.'

'Why shouldn't you?'

'Because he's not a Christian – and I suppose it's wrong for me to do the things he and his group do.'

'Well, let's deal with you first,' Paul said, 'but whether or not Steve is a Christian isn't necessarily a reason to avoid him.'

'Why can't I just forget Mr Kennedy?'

'Because you've helped to do him wrong and you feel guilty. The fact that nobody knows makes it even worse, doesn't it?'

'Yes.'

Paul grinned, 'Well, it was stupid, but you know that

now. You got caught up in a situation and you weren't quite strong enough to resist going along with the crowd. You've paid for it in sleepless nights I guess!'

Rachel nodded.

'What can I do?' she asked miserably.

Paul sat back in his chair and screwed up his eyes as if trying to find a solution. He remained like this for some moments then abruptly leaned forward.

'You must write to Mr Kennedy and explain what happened. You must say sorry for your part in the incident.'

'Oh no, I couldn't!' Rachel exclaimed. She had dreaded Paul suggesting something like that. Just telling them both had been bad enough. If only he had given her a stern ticking off and left it at that – but this! It was too much to ask. Paul, however, was adamant.

'It's the only way, Rachel. You haven't hurt *me*, it's Mr Kennedy you've injured. He's the person who must be apologised to.'

'What if he's really angry with me and won't accept my being sorry?' Rachel argued.

'My guess is that he'll be impressed with your decision to own up. Anyway, Rachel, it's not his response that's important, it's the fact that you've done the right thing. You'll never feel really peaceful about the matter until you've made amends – and this is the only way.'

Rachel frowned rebelliously, looking for a way out, but Paul was determined.

'OK. I'll do it,' she said sullenly after several minutes had elapsed.

'You won't regret it, Rachel.'

'Would I have to tell Mum, do you think?'

Paul smiled at her. 'I think the letter will do for now. If at some time in the future you can tell your mum, well, that might be a good thing, but you'll have done your part once the letter is written. Then you can put it behind you and stop worrying.'

'It should never have happened in the first place,' Rachel said gloomily.

'Don't say that, Rachel. We all do things we regret – even when we think we're older and wiser! It's not the mistakes that God minds so much as what we do with them afterwards. No matter what we've done, God is only too willing to forgive us when we turn back to him, tell him our sins and ask for his help in making a fresh start. He doesn't expect us to manage on our own.'

Rachel smiled. She felt very tired and very relieved. It was so good to have the whole stupid incident out in the open. When she got home she'd write the letter. It wouldn't be easy but it would be in the post tomorrow, without fail, she promised herself. Funny, but it didn't seem like a huge problem at all now.

'More coffee, everybody?' Liz asked brightly and Rachel nodded gratefully. Paul had to go out soon afterwards but Liz invited Rachel to stay and help her staple some cut-out figures together which she was getting ready for the infants' class at church.

'What's Steve like, then? That's his name, isn't it?' she enquired after they'd worked for a bit, just chatting generally.

'Oh, he's nice,' Rachel began hesitantly. 'Not like his mates really, at least I don't think so. He just doesn't think about things sometimes.'

'What things?'

'Well, like whether it's right to do something or not – I suppose the boat incident is a good example. He just didn't know why I was getting so worried. He made me feel really childish. But I know he's not mean or rough.'

'I'm sure he's not. There must be some good qualities in him that you were attracted by.'

'Oh there are, Liz,' Rachel enthused. 'He's funny, and he's really concerned about people – well, some of them, anyway.'

'And he didn't want you to get into trouble – that shows a lot, doesn't it?'

'Yes, it does.'

'So,' Liz said casually, 'what are you going to do about him?'

'I still like him, and I shouldn't . . .'

'Being a Christian certainly doesn't mean we pick and choose our friends – quite the opposite,' Liz stated.

'But Vanessa kept saying he'd get me into trouble – and she was right. Why couldn't I see that?'

'Things may not be as black and white as Vanessa says.'

'What shall I do, Liz?'

'What do you want to do?'

'To see him again, but not like last time when I just wanted to go along with the group. I want my relationship with God to come first but I don't know how.'

'You've just said it, Rachel. If you keep putting God first, you won't make the same mistakes. That means talking to God, as a trusted friend and as your Lord, every day. Read your Bible and ask questions so that you learn more about his will for you. Don't rely on your own strength and will – God wants to give you his gifts of peace and joy, and to provide you with his strength. Do you understand?'

'I think I'm beginning to.'

'For a start, you should tell your mum about Steve. It's not right to deceive her. And it's no good trying to lead a double life – one when you're with Steve and his friends, the other when you're at church. God wants you to be his person all the time – which is a lot easier in the long run!'

Rachel grinned. 'Yes, I've found that out.'

'It's not necessary yet to think about the future, but for now any friendship with Steve has to be based on honesty and respect. He mustn't change you or make you compromise what you believe. If that happens, you are turning your back on God. The laughs will turn to regrets and tears. As a Christian, you have the privilege to witness for God.'

'What does that really mean?'

'It means showing Steve and his friends that you're different – not in a freaky or judging way – but by quietly, firmly, standing up for what is good and loving, as Jesus did, and not being afraid to talk about what you believe.'

'How can I make Steve become a Christian? I want him to be one now that I'm beginning to see how much it means.'

Liz laughed. 'Always in such a hurry, aren't you? You can't make people love God. He wouldn't want that in any case, because he's made us free. God is overjoyed when we freely turn to him. As a witness, you can tell others about Jesus, and your life shows them about him. That's a real responsibility, but ultimately only the Holy Spirit gives them their own relationship with God.'

'I see.' Rachel was thinking with shame of the sort of witness she had been so far – self-interested, angry, unforgiving. Oh dear, there was a long way to go. She had always thought it was enough just not to deny that you went to church. But at least now she had something real to talk about. She knew God was her friend.

'Don't worry,' Liz said, guessing her thoughts. 'God doesn't expect us to be perfect; only to try.'

'Will Steve understand?'

'That's something you must talk about. If Steve doesn't accept you on those terms . . .'

'I know. I'll have to make a choice. I know what choice to make now, though.'

'I'm so glad, Rachel. It's wonderful to see you so sure about your faith. You've had to struggle for a while, haven't you?'

'Yes,' Rachel said simply. 'I suppose I liked some bits of being a Christian but not others. Now I know that what I do *does* matter; people matter and there are consequences to think about. I also thought I wanted more fun and excitement. Now, I realise that God wants me to have fun too and being a Christian is the most exciting thing! Funny I couldn't see that!'

'God loves you as you are, Rachel, don't forget that. A bit of finding out for yourself does no harm. It makes your relationship with God more personal.'

Rachel and Liz returned to the cardboard pieces energetically. Rachel had some hard thinking to do. She was determined to tell her mum about Steve as soon as possible, so there would be no more lying and covering up to do. She had to see Steve too, and there was the difficult letter to write. But it felt so good to feel the knot of problems and troubles unravelling and melting away. Her only surprise was that it had taken so much anxiety before she'd found the way out. Why on earth hadn't she asked God to help sooner!

11

It was over a week later that Rachel bumped into Sue at school in the girls' cloakroom. She had hardly seen any of the group since that awful assembly and had almost given up looking for an opportunity to speak to Steve on his own. He seemed to be avoiding her.

Sue was flicking up her new punk hairstyle when she spotted Rachel and immediately turned to face her.

'Hi there! Not seen you for a while.'

'Oh, hello. No, I've been busy with coursework so I've been in the library at lunch times.'

'Someone's been looking for you,' Sue said, ignoring the explanation.

'Who?' Rachel asked blankly.

'He rides a bike – used to be a friend of yours, I thought.'

'Steve?' Rachel breathed, as a tiny knot started forming in her stomach.

'Yeah, that's his name. He wants you to know he'll be outside the metalwork room after school.'

'Oh, thanks!' Rachel stammered.

'Just thought you'd like to know!' Sue called back over her shoulder as she departed.

Rachel saw him first. He was leaning against the fire door with his hands in his pockets, trying to look as though he always waited there after school. Rachel couldn't help smiling. He was embarrassed, just as she had been once before. Strange, but she felt quite calm now.

'Waiting for someone?' Rachel said, as he looked up and noticed her. Her eyes sparkled with amusement.

'Maybe,' he returned, unsure of himself.

'I've been wanting to talk to you,' Rachel said.

'Me too.'

'I wanted to say sorry about being so rude the other day.'

'Forget it. I know how you felt about that evening. It wasn't meant to end like that.'

Rachel sighed. Did he mean being found out, or all of it? Was he really sorry?

'I wrote to Mr Kennedy,' she continued.

'Yes, I know.'

'Oh! But how?'

'I'm working for him, remember?'

'Of course.' Rachel hesitated but she had to continue. 'Do you know why I wrote? I mean, after keeping my name out of it, you must have wondered what on earth I was doing.'

'At first I was puzzled, but then I realised, it was just the sort of thing you would do. Christians have a thing about confessing, don't they?' Steve teased.

'You're making fun!' Rachel felt annoyed.

'Did you know you have a real temper! I thought Christians were supposed to be quiet and calm."

'Not all the time,' she retorted.

'Seriously though, I do understand – about having to say sorry. When I started working on the boat with Mr Kennedy, I realised how much it means to him. I felt a rat for wasting all his hard work. I knew how I'd have felt if it had been my bike.'

Rachel nodded. She was so thankful that he understood.

'Shall we walk?' Rachel said.

'Yeah.'

They moved off slowly, a little apart but there was no tension. It felt good to be together. A gentle breeze rippled their hair and the afternoon sun stretched long shadows before them.

'I've got an invitation for you,' Steve said after a while.

'Who from?'

'Mr Kennedy.'

Rachel's eyes widened in surprise.

'He wants you to come and see the *Lady Caroline* when we've finished her.'

'Seriously?'

'Yes, he's mentioned it twice now. I said I'd ask you.'

'He wants me to see the boat!' Rachel repeated incredulously.

'That's right.'

'I don't think so. How on earth can I ever face the man again after . . . ?'

'I had to,' Steve reminded her.

'Yes, well, that's different. You've been helping him to put right the damage.'

'So have you. He was pretty impressed with your letter – showed it to me. It made things a lot easier for me, too. He stopped going on about "the youth of today" all the time. I think he'd be really pleased if you came down to see the boat – sort of show you were interested.'

'Well, maybe I could. Yes, I suppose it would be OK,' Rachel said, warming to the idea. It would set the seal on things somehow.

'I wouldn't want to go on my own though,' she added.

'You could come down with me one evening,' Steve suggested tentatively, 'if you like.'

'Yes, maybe,' she returned.

They had reached the park which bordered Rachel's estate and found themselves entering the sombre iron gates. The swings and roundabouts were clearing as young children were hauled off home by mums or older brothers and sisters. Rachel and Steve headed for an empty bench facing the slide. It seemed only a short time ago that Rachel would have been scrambling up the ladder with Vanessa, laughing and fooling about. Funny how you suddenly grew up, Rachel thought, and how life became more complicated. As if reading her thoughts, Steve spoke.

'So where do we go from here?' he said. 'Is there any future for us?'

'I'm not sure.'

'Thanks a bunch!' he laughed awkwardly.

'I like you,' Rachel said simply.

'I like you too.'

'But there are other things to consider. Other people, and God.'

'I see.'

'Do you really?' Rachel was in earnest now.

'You're not going to stay around if I go off the straight and narrow?' Steve joked.

'I'm not messing around, Steve.'

'I'm sorry.'

They were silent for a while.

'You see, I'm beginning to realise how important God is to me and that's going to affect all sorts of things in the future.'

'Do you regret getting to know me?'

'Oh no, of course not. In a funny way I suppose that disastrous evening was good for me.'

'I've never been called a disaster before!' Steve laughed. 'It's different anyway.'

'It wasn't you!'

'It was partly. You wouldn't have been "led astray" if you hadn't been with me.'

'But I've got to stand by my own decisions. All I cared about when I first met you, was trying to be one of the gang.'

'I didn't ask you to be like the others!'

'I know! That's what was so stupid of me.'

'I suppose it's what we all do, though – try to be one of the crowd, whichever crowd we're with.'

'Yes, that's it exactly!' Rachel cried, pleased that he understood. 'But we don't have to be. God loves us just as we are and if he wants us to change, it's for our own happiness, not to make us fit into some mould.'

'It's important to you, isn't it, what you believe in?'

'Yes, it is.'

'Look, Rachel, I know you're different from any girl I've ever been out with before and I've told you that I'm glad about that. I'm interested in why you go to church and I'd like you to tell me about it some day, but I can't promise I'm going to become a Christian too, just to make it all right between us. I don't know if I believe in it, or if I ever will. I'm sorry.'

'Don't be sorry. You've been honest – that's all I want, for both of us.'

'Does that make it impossible for us to see each other?'

'No,' Rachel murmured. A moment later she felt his hand squeeze hers.

'I promise I'll respect the things you believe in. I hope you can accept me as I am.'

'I will,' Rachel proclaimed solemnly.

Sitting there, holding hands, the whispered words sounded so serious that they laughed, embarrassed.

'Hey, I've got an invitation for you too!' Rachel announced, breaking the spell.

'Go on.'

'Will you come to the youth club barbecue on Friday evening? We're meeting outside the church hall at seven thirty. I'd like you to meet some of my friends.'

'What about tonight? We could go for a ride again, on our own.'

Rachel hesitated for the briefest second.

'No thanks, I promised I'd go sketching with Vanessa tonight.'

'Oh yes, you've got exams coming up haven't you? OK then, Friday it is.'

'Great!'

'And now . . . what about doing something really daring and exciting?'

'Like what?' Rachel said, with a worried frown. Whatever was he planning now?

'Bet you can't beat me to the top of that slide!'

Rachel's mouth dropped open and then she laughed.

'You idiot! Wait for me,' she screamed as he tore off across the tarmac.

'Do you know what we must look like!' she gasped as they landed in a giggling heap at the bottom.

'Who cares!" he grinned, helping her up. "We're free, we're young and life's great!'

'Do you want to walk me home?' Rachel asked.

'Yeah.'

'Catch me then.' And she darted away with Steve on her heels, both of them screaming like kids.